Condemned to Cymru

AN
ACHRONOLOGICAL
ABECEDARIAN
PICARESQUE

M.J. Nicholls

© 2022 by M.J. Nicholls

All Rights Reserved.

Set in Mrs Eaves XL with LaTeX.

ISBN: 978-1-952386-24-4 (paperback)
ISBN: 978-1-952386-25-1 (ebook)
Library of Congress Control Number: 2021944633

Sagging Meniscus Press
Montclair, New Jersey
saggingmeniscus.com

CONTENTS

In Which the Blemished Are Banished   1

Condemned to Cymru   9

Helga Horsedòttir   195

CONDEMNED TO CYMRU

In Which the Blemished Are Banished

I WAS HARD AT WORK popping two Quantum IV pimples when I heard Hottdóttirish hobnails on hardwood. It was Katrin Hottdóttir in her ear-shredding hobnail boots, her laddered tights and ill-faced tortoiseshell specs clomping towards me with an air of pleasant menace. Her thin chapped lips were about to mouth words pre-mouthed two minutes thence from the managerial menagerie—Aron Bergþóruson, Gunnar Bergþóruson, and Viktor Bergþóruson—the beaming brotherhood of The Húsavík Research Hive, where I worked as a pimple-popping basement operative unsackable because of laws.

"Hey, Magnus. We're having a cake moment in the vestibule," she said. I spied a Battenberg crumb on her lower lip. I wanted to munch Battenberg in the vestibule. However, I suffered from a level of acne known to dermatologists as "post-post-nuclear", so I could not munch. I had a lunar face populated with a series of inverted craters, like an exploding moon. The once smooth pink skin of childhood had been blitzed by little ball bearings that itched and bled and wept pus from time to time, usually whenever I wanted to interact with another human being, and I had to wear four layers of makeup to appear presentable. I wanted to eat Battenberg in the vestibule, however, The Húsavík Research Hive—a cornerstone of the New Icelandic commitment to appearing young and sexually irresistible at all times—frowned on the unsexable mutations of genetic mishaps, and kept us from view as reminders of a past of inbreeding. "It is constitutionally inappropriate, Katrin, that I should eat cake," I replied.

"What?"

"I'll pass."

"The brotherhood would like a word," she added.

"Now?"

I had spent the morning as usual thinking up schemes to make Iceland appear more smug on the world stage. I took an hour writing a report on the influence of Icelandic avant-pop literature on the next wave of *New Yorker* writers, then an hour teasing the pus from a Quantum IV (I might explain the various pimple classifications later), to bring the altitude to a manageable level, and with a little blusher, reduce the beast to a Quantum II. I took the backstairs to the elevator, up to the top floor bubble-office that the brothers shared—a conceptual pimple on the smirking mug of the Research Hive.

"Magnus! A proposition?" Head One said. The Bergþóruson brothers were a three-headed enigma of cocoa-brown backcombing and designer pince-nez. I perched on the edge of a bubble chair, angled at their preferred 42°.

"Sure."

The Húsavík Research Hive was formed following Iceland's successful transformation of Brunei from a self-serving sultanate into a collectivist Viking monoculture in order to fatten our influence in corrupt outcrops. Since the last two pandemoniums in America and Europe, most war-whomped nations sought workable solutions to help postpone the next one. Iceland had produced a catalogue—*Bloodbath Alternatives: Building Your Country's Wealth Without Butchery*. The Hive was formed as part of an award-winning PR assault on the world, showcasing Iceland as the most vibrant and arousing nation unbothered with slime-ridden autocrats and sex pests. I was hired to help scheme up further means of larding Viking love into the Earth's pores after I submitted several notions to the Bergþórusons, including the introduction of webcams in the echelons of power, so the public could hear what their leaders were scheming, removing all distrust between voter and politician. I was co-opted into the Hive in spite of the frothing tumult of acne on my otherwise exceptionally acceptable face, and allowed an office. Having solved the bulk of the world's ecological and political problems with the simple rubric of not behaving like insane nitwits, The Hive concentrated on a range of innovative nonstick notions such as installing tip-meters next to the homeless to prevent passersby from having to lean over to deposit coins in a cup; installing chip pans with a heat-sensor that alerted the fire brigade to an unacceptable temperature in someone's kitchen; and a special silencer on a bathroom hand drier to prevent unwanted ear damage in the drying of one's mitts.

"We have appraised your cerebral transmissions and think you are the right person to helm our new Cultural Excavation Exhibition," Head Two said. "As we know, the war between Liechtenstein and Wales was catastrophic for the United Kingdom. The country was carpet-bombed and pumped with bullets and smashed up something bad. All traces of the former cultural life there have vanished from world awareness."

"Yes, it was in the news."

"And they had some problems with chemical leaks and weird mutations and stuff."

"Yes. News."

"This is an unmissable opportunity for Iceland to shape the nascent culture of the ravaged United Kingdom," said Head Three. "It is probable that Iceland will colonise that country shortly, after Timor-Leste, Bulgaria, and Comoros, so we would like someone to bring us reports on the Welsh people—their culture, their beliefs, their Weltanschauungs—to help smooth our Icelandic-British alliance and herald in the new era of that nation with us in charge. This is, of course, several years away."

I had to smile (although smiling made my philtric pimple poke into my right nostril, and emerge with an unlovely sheen of cold mucus, so I never smiled). This was a diplomatic deportation strategy.

"Continue," I invited.

"We would like you to collect information and compile reports on every village or town you visit. We are asking you to bumblebee one of the most significant tasks this hive has ever buzzed. As you know, it is our mission to spread the warm butter of Iceland across the ciabatta of the universe, from our folk dancing, our novels about sheep farmers, and our sense of resentful yet industrious binding of community. You will continue this fine tradition across your long and exhaustive travels."

"Clever. You have found a means at last of oust."

"Pardon?"

"I understand. I am a son of a son of a son of a Magnussonson. I have inherited what has been termed 'contrasocially problemsome facial grievances', or as I prefer, 'a fuckhaul of purulent spots and pimples that seep hard'. My ancestors, in particular my grandfather's grandfather squared, or if you prefer, Magnussonson[4], suffered from one of the most legendary blemishes in Icelandic history. His infamous boil, Popocatepetl, began on his fat chin, and over the course of a lifetime, subsumed his entire visage, so that when he turned fifty, he was little more than a boil-headed freakshow as snoggable as The Elephant Man. He was condemned to view the suppurating inner world of his head-boil, making long, haunting moans from a mouth inflummoxed with über-rasped skin. Having missed his chance to commit suicide, clinging for decades to the hope that a prominent surgeon might rescue him from his in-fallen face, he was sentenced to walking around blind, unable to locate bridges from which to leap. I have glommed some of that particular genetic repugnance, and you can't tolerate this in your sexy orb."

"This is not a discrimination thing," Head ??? said.

After a few months, the Icelandic Dream had a strong Aryan whiff. Organisations began to remove their blemished from view, pushing us into basement offices, sealed cubicles, and outbuildings several hectares from the site. At The Hive, I was the relocated to subterranean premises with a wall-mounted sink. Next came Kristin Harr, with the unwaxable upper lip, a victim of a rare hormone imbalance that caused an hourly reprise of her partial moustache. No one wished to see such feminine hair over their lunchtime bowl of kimchi noodlettes on flatbread. Then followed Michael Growther, cursed with a reverse hump protruding from his left adenoid, and Salman Victor, with an outbending foot that tripped up runners and pizza people, and Lorna Oost, an albino with a purplish pigment in her right eyeball, and Chad Tee, an unattractive man with a clavicle wart. This sad persecution of the unpretty unlolled like a corpse's tongue into the stinking fart-bucket of the conscience-free Icelandic populous.

"So my eminently reasonable assertion that a hereditary skin condition that even the loftiest quacks of Icelandic medicine cannot treat is somehow in contra with our new airbrushed image is complete nonsense?"

The Bergþórusons were silent for a moment.

"We think this will be a nice experience for you. It might help uncrease some of the vulgarities in your character. Take your lady with you to Wales. All expenses paid. Have fun, Magnus. Email us your reports."

I hurled pants and unguents into a suitcase. I saw my cat Lionel Shriver off to the cattery. I convinced my rancid girlfriend Katrin to come along. I went to Wales, I bummed around Wales, I came back from Wales, and I handed in my "reports", in alphabetical order, to my paymasters.

Condemned to Cymru

Aberbargoed
Translated, means "half-lost in the pocket of a worsted trouser".

Abercastle
Helga Horsedóttir, for you, I would help a narked parker insinuate herself between two Jeeps.

Aberffraw
I see: a montage of pale-skinned women wincing at a plethora of long-popped pimples.

Abergele
Look, I am undecuntable. It is otherwise impossible. I am a permanent scowl on legs.

Abergwynfi
In a hell-red West Glamorgan haze, in off-white fit stretch chinos, I ponder the meaning of the phrase "you screechy rustic hellcat".

Abergwyngregyn
Make no mistake, the slow, eventual release of a burp following an intake of carbonated water is one of the finest things in life.

Abergynolwyn
Translated, means "voted hard inside a Lutheran exit poll".

Aberllefenni
No pavements.

Aberkenfig
I was having a nice time lawnbowling until I remembered Idi Amin.

Abertysswg
The most insipid circle of hell is soundtracked by Aztec Camera.

Adfa

'Brilliant Brian' from Barrie Bartmel's *Poems of a Poltroon* (p.38):

> Bound inside the latex banana
> the brilliant Brian stepped forth.
>
> He swerved along the ledge and winked
> as the winds went into updraught.

Afon Wen

"An étude on the perils of writing?" Vaughan Grenade asked me in an unnamed bar.

"No," I replopped.

"I will begin. I once wrote a story. When I began this story, I had six friends. In the first draft the protagonist was Michael Vincent Smith, the managing director of Clarks for the East Lothian region. The plot centred around Michael's fear that the shoe-shop chain might become obsolete in the region due to the harsh economic reality that people were too poor to buy shoes directly from a retailer—it was cheaper to source second-hand (or second-foot) shoes from £1 shops or branches of Oxfam. The story ended with Michael stepping down from his position as managing director after a nervous breakdown.

"I showed this story to my friend Michael Vincent Smith, the managing director for Clarks in the West Lothian region who had recently had a nervous breakdown due to economic pressures. He explained that the story took certain aspects of his life that he wasn't comfortable being made public. I told him I had changed his location from East to West Lothian and that should be sufficient to protect his identity. I also explained no one would likely read this story, since I was an obscure writer unpublished by major presses or magazines. He wasn't satisfied and threatened to end our friendship if I continued with the story. I stuck to my artistic guns. We parted as enemies.

"After receiving a threatening legal document from Michael I rewrote the story around a couple, Sara and Bob Fenton, two cake decorators from Niddrie who caught diphtheria on holiday last year. My story was about two cake directors from Riddrie who, etc. I pleaded with them to remain in the story, but legal documents were issued yet again. My three remaining friends were part of a Bulgarian soccer team. In 2009 they won a local tournament, let the success get to their heads, and ended up sacked from the squad for taking too much heroin on the pitch. I put them into the third draft, to the same outcome.

"I now have no friends, no one to write about, and no story to tell."

Albro Castle

Barrie Bartmel received one lukewarm review for his collection *Poems of a Poltroon* in his lifetime in a handwritten college zine. Now that he is a corpse, his poems are being embroidered onto teatowels. Take note, scribblers.

Alltwen

"Marketing algorithms will never understand me," Katrin said. "I search on purpose for things I have no intention of buying. A roof rack for a Range Rover Evoque. A microplane premium lemon zester with a blood orange handle. The poetry of Rod McKuen. A signed portrait of the actor James Caan. Your pathetic attempts to understand me through soulless algorithms merely reflects your own failure to grasp the complexity of my staggeringly baffling and unfathomable mental cave."

Alltyblacca

From *An Alternative History of Wales*:

189 BC: The spoon is invented in Pentregwenlais.

100 BC: Lies that there are not enough hillforts to house all the immigrants result in 6,000 beheadings.

48 AD: Romans arrive and use Wales to store their excess zinc.

Amlwch

Bergþórusons, one morning the benumbed bourgeois will rise from their riverside condos and take to the streets with machetes, looking for the triad of corporate scoundrels who have boxed them into lives of art-house films on Cambodian sex slaves, £9.99 cappuccinos that show their haggard faces in foam, and wailing tots force-fed lentils strapped to papooses. The sound of your necks snapping is the sound of freedom.

Amroth
Katrin said her pimpliness had made her crazed with lust. She was riddled with paranoia that attractive people were shagging more than her and in her desperation to live a youth of rampant sexual abandon, she would hurl herself at middle-aged weirdoes from all walks of life.

Argoed
Katrin: "My auntie said to me, 'If this were the Victorian era, I would hurl your stripling ass into the Danube, pivot forth and huff *I have no daughter*. Alas, this is the modern era so I have to accept your hereness.'"

Axton Hill
I swear I saw the staggered apparition of William F. Buckley coming over the hill.

Badminton
I first met Katrin at a bus stop. "You're a repulsive freak like me," she said. I smiled.

Bala
An elbow ate my tagliatelle.

Bancffosfelen
If the concept of tweeness became a republic, and that republic was populated by the closest human encapsulations of tweeness, like a thousand Zooey Deschanel clones, and that republic required a national anthem to promote the proud tweeness of the nation, that national anthem would be provided by Belle & Sebastian.

Bancyfelin

Translated, means "long surgical procedure involving a conch".

Bangor-on-Dee

I observed a frown-faced teen at a bus stop. I sketched a brief yawp from his sullen mind. Whenever a comedian made witty observations about the day-to-day stuff of life, he'd chuckle along as though a part of that collective understanding. As though he too knew how long girls took in the bathroom, or how hard it was to get served at the bar if you were a short-arse, when he'd never had a girlfriend or been to a bar because every muscle in his body would freeze up outside adult buildings and he'd spend thirty minutes pacing up and down the streets trying to will himself to go in. Because what if they didn't like him? What if they saw him and laughed at his gauche inadequacy, saw right through his pretence of being one of them and watched as he humiliated himself into a corner, stuttering and spluttering until his head exploded with embarrassment? Would he ever leave his bedroom again, attempt to make conversation with anyone? But what frightened him most, what he suspected to be true, was that there was no "they" in pubs or clubs or adult buildings, there were only a series of thems, groups of pre-established friends who stood around pointing at weirdoes, weirdoes like him, pointing out all those who didn't conform to their own notions of casual coolness, of detached irony and precocious emotional maturity. And whenever he saw himself inside those buildings, with those attractive sweaty happy people, drinking their drinks, dancing their dances, he saw himself standing at the door, hunched like a twisted old doorman, waiting for someone to speak to him and show him the way to happiness, knowing no one would approach him other than asking him to leave for skulking around the door like a weirdo, and then he'd never ever ever go back there ever again. And he wished they'd die a thousand deaths for taking their happiness from a youth culture that alienated him so much he felt like his own grandfather, when he should have been spending his youth raving it up in this fast, noisy, careless world, and taking what every other boy his age was free to take: a world of colours, lust, sensations and pleasure.

Bargoed
Translated, means "the end of shrubbery in the United Kingdom".

Beaufort
I am flatpacked into paranoia. Last night I saw twelve balloons in the corner, rising from the carpet and blowing bum notes into the night, like strangled trombones, as I sat trembling on the frozen sheets, listening to an orchestra of popping parps in the autumnal clutches of this backwater. I am working hard not to fall into madman clichés. I have an overwhelming urge to hump a tractor. Who has water?

Beaumaris
You have to admire the sticking power of Ace of Base. Following the surprise hit of their paean to esurient motherhood, 'All that She Wants', a song that encapsulated the brooding frustrations for a generation of late-twentysomething unwed and unsexed women and, conversely, a generation of seedless male hangers-on wondering at what exact point their untrammelled lust morphed into the sour hours of childless aggro, the Swedish foursome might have pocketed their profits and settled into breezy lives compèring child talent contents in Malmö. Instead, the unit powered on through three mediocre albums, and in 2010, had the chutzpah to relaunch with younger, sexier female vocalists next to the pot-bellied and beefcaked co-founders Ulf and Jonas. Ace of Base were the true spirit of Europop—sprightly, hilariously sincere, and oddly likeable.

Beddgelert
"Have you ever loved anything?" Katrin asked.

"I almost loved my father when he patted my head twice after I received my anthropology degree. The bravery in overcoming his hard-coded affectlessness seemed, in that moment, a rare signifier of fatherly love. Then, on reflection, I realised it absolutely fucking wasn't, that it was absolutely fucking pathetic, and I went back to being me."

Bedwellty
I met Katrin the second time at an Einstürzende Neubauten concert. Her German pronunciation was faultless.

Begelly
Giraffes and anthracite.

Benllech
Burped hard in Tesco.

Bethania
Father: "Pass me the plokkfiskur, son."

Bethesda
In that way that two lurchy middle-aged males lock mental antlers over a surplus of hops, and those two males swing from bar to bar, hop-tippling until the bitter bombast of their mutual spleen lapses into belchy nonspecific slurs on women and ex-bosses, I ended up on Daffid Costa's couch, staring at a large fissure in the man's anus, where a lump of shrapnel had wedged seven months prior, ripping that part of his poophole free. I stared at the scabbed stitching running around the contours of his bellicosely enhanced exit as he said: "I will personally slaughter—*hic!*—every one of those Liechtensteinian asswombats. I will not rest until the whole of Liechtenstein lies dead beneath my—*hic!*—sword."

Bettws Cedewain
This is what Callum Overwish said to me:
 "I regret nothing, you slavering mongrels. Sure, I sat around on my moth-eaten sofa, reading Chaucer, reading Dostoevsky, reading Dickens, while you sat punching stats into a Mac for your hateful paymasters. I sat writing my unauthorised novels while sipping milkshakes and munching Malteasers, while you navigated a forklift truck across

a warehouse so a fat prick in a boardroom could make a million extra bucks. You made your choices, you swine, and I made mine. And you, the sour-faced embittered masses, you chose to persecute *me*, a man who longed for something more than this oneclick consumerist bog of a civilisation we have built for ourselves, this predatory playground in which we pulverise each other for a better house, a faster car, and a safe, substanceless future. I chose to enrich my mind and my soul with literature, you cowering flocculents, at the expense of material things. I made myself an exile to money, a traitor to the capitalist cause, and you shunned me. So swept up in yourselves, so miserable with your state-approved struggles, you looked to me, a man bewildered by the cutthroat cash-obsessed world who, to cope with the anxiety and paranoia at being boxed inside this drama of exile, retreated into a world of the imagination, and you chose to bully and humiliate me, and cast me into the wilds, because I showed you a mirror of the person you never had the courage, or pig-headed defiance to become. Lock me up, you fascists of boredom. Incarcerate me, you tyrants of tedium. I am always free in my own mind."

Betws
If I had to sum up Katrin in two words, those words would be "petulant" and "unclean".

Betws Gwerfil Goch
There was a rumour (spread by the middle Bergþóruson) that the middle Bergþóruson had slept with Björk Guðmundsdóttir. No one sleeps with Björk. She is an impermeable fortress of post-human wonderment.

Betws Ifan
If this village were a sentence, that sentence would be "Maggots emerged from the toddler's gangrenous wound".

Betws yn Rhos
Whenever I wamble into hell, I like to nibble on a colourful fruit. The tears streaming up, my soul wedged hard into a rotting bucket of horror, I sit at a table, sucking the pulp of a papaya. The contrast between my scabby tear-sodden head of skin and the sun-yellow South American fruit, as the bright succulent pieces are shoved between my blubbering lips, is so ludicrous, that I am slowly coddled in the reassuring arms of absurdity and futility, my two surrogate mothers. I now have enough willpower to take a shower.

Blackwood
I watched a beautiful couple eating salad in an artisan bistro with their airbrushed spawn. It consoled me to think of them as wrinkled cadavers being lowered into the muck. O, the unstoppable cudgelling of time, how I love thee.

Blaenau Ffestiniog
I stood atop a knoll and looked at this historic mining town and thought on the staggering progress we have made as a species, from bog to bluetooth, and wondered if perhaps our imaginations and intelligence might rescue us from the oncoming stampede of thundercunts seeking to extinguish all traces of enlightened thought. I wondered if it was possible that light might triumph over darkness when the Great Fireball descended. Then I remembered Rob Schneider. I drowned the thought in a sack and spat into the wind.

Blaenawey
A tractor was once seen here.

Blaenporth
When Katrin's tongue is on my penis, I am the living embodiment of the word "disappointment".

Blaenrhondda
A legal firm introduced a new claim for victims of social embarrassment. Bo Moore visited the firm of Creaker & Weeper after a humiliat-

ing time spent at The Sock & Muppet pub on Blaen Avenue, claiming that he had been "traumatised" after an incident by a pub user who accosted him on various topics on which he was ill-equipped to speak such as the NASDAQ and the films of Andrei Tarkovsky, resulting in awkward silence among a crowd of his intellectual superiors, and his inevitable humiliated retreat from the pub. The client sued the pub for not placing a sign out front reading: "Possible risk of social embarrassment." If this sign had been placed outside the pub, the client would not have suffered such a dramatic setback to his social life (two months without leaving the flat followed), nor needed to sue the pub for £10,000. Thereafter all businesses in the village bore the sign: CAUTION! SOCIAL EMBARRASSMENT. ENTER AT YOUR OWN RISK. The legal firm sued five more businesses before dropping their new claim as unprofitable. (This might not have happened.)

Blaina
Translated, means "pub with no publicans currently alive".

Bodewryd
Horses and the dead.

Bodfari
Translated, means "shortness in the long term is pathetic."

Bodffordd
Translated, means "an aeroplane propellor in a bucket of llama guts."

Bodior
Some places aren't a place.

Boncath
If it came to light that Barrie Bartmel faked his own death, the media would stop praising his poems and condemn him for misleading people into thinking his work had no merit because he was alive.

Bont Dolgadfan
Yes, I poured warm custard into a saxophone.

Bont Pren
I am the unvarnished stoat of relinquishment.

Bontddu
A pub and a goldmine.

Bontuchel
Sometimes I worry when I am shovelling carbs into my maw that I am happiest when I am thinking precisely nothing, and that thoughts are the enemy of human contentment, and that I have already ruined everything by thinking something for the first time as a newborn.

Borth
This is what Eleanor Cart said to me:
"In little under three decades of existence, Eleanor Cart—that's I—had earned herself the oxymoronic moniker The Living Corpse. This referred to her fondness for excessive sleep and loafing in bed to prevent the onslaught of the new morning (or afternoon, or evening). In truth, she found the moniker more depressing than the fact of her fondness for excessive sleep, and this source of sorrow ended up lengthening the time she might have otherwise spent preparing to arise from her bed to confront the clock. This was not the lone example of a caustic moniker intended to lighten a depression deepening the depression instead. Previous monikers included The Butter Ball, after Guy de Maupassant's story *Boule de suif*, chosen for her copious butter consumption between the period of October 2013 and March 2014, causing a spell of excessive self-awareness and depression about her weight increase; The Grease Lightnin', chosen to poke fun at her short period of abstaining to wash her hair, prolonged from two to nine months; and The Madness of King George, chosen upon recognising certain mannerisms shared between herself and Nigel Hawthorne's King George during the onset of dementia stage. Eleanor Cart—that's

I—resembled a more bedraggled version of Ludelle Black from 1990s garage rock outfit Thee Headcoatees, circa 1999, after the release of the *Here Comes Cessation* LP."

Bosherton

People tell me this place looked presentable in 1944.

Boughrood (Bochrwd)

Helga Horsedóttir, for you, I would appear as a witness in the trial of a rage-cheeked ex-marine who burned his turtle with cigarillos.

Boulston

Helga Horsedóttir, for you, I would compliment a falconer on the exquisite plumage of her sharp-shinned hawk (as it swooped across the Keswick distance).

Boverton

I awake in the inclement throb of a summer's apse.

Bradley

I am ashamed.

Britannia

Once, in an attempt to make our willed coupling less repulsive, Katrin and I tried sex wearing the masks of more promising people. For missionary, I was Gerard Butler, she Laura Dern. For on-top, I was John Hamm, she Penelope Cruz. For doggie style, I was Liam Neeson, she Melanie Griffith. Unfortunately, this cardboard recasting only fortified our spotty unloveableness, our pockmarked crater-faced disgustingness, and wilted our mutual libidos. Since that mistake, we always have sex looking straight into each other's eyes. That way we can reach honest, delusion-free climaxes, and slither away with an illusion of self-respect.

Brithdir

On an undisturbed, picturesque stretch of land with nothing man-made for miles, I stopped to let the cool breeze caress me, and take meditative breaths in the generous heart of nature. I realised that someone, somewhere, would see this land and think: "I could build a fucking massive supermarket here." The moment was ruined.

Brithdir Mawr

Translated, means "immolated in aspic".

Briton Ferry

In some respects, basing our relationship on a mutual resentment has kept it stronger. We are able to express the frequent feelings of utter loathing we have towards one another without letting them bubble under the surface. It is common for us to spit venom in the morning and screw with abandon in the evening.

Broadfield

I was so not interested in the residents of Broadfield. I had to creep towards this small village like a mutineer walking the plank. I could not have been more blinkered. Carolanne's crème brûlée was outstanding. Tom the welder's savage satirical humour was refreshing. Yolande's origami reenactments of Boer War episodes were award-winning. Come, one and all, to the sainted dominion of Broadfield!

Bronant

'The Time of Shafting' from Barrie Bartmel's *Poems of a Poltroon* (p.20):

> I spend my weekdays in fear
> of those brown HMRC envelopes
> falling through the letterbox
> informing me that today
> is my time to be shafted in the rear
>
> And I spend my weekdays in fear
> of those phonecalls

       from stern medics in dark rooms
       informing me that today
       my lover has been shafted in the rear

       And I spend my weekdays in fear
       of those emails and texts
       from those at the scene
       informing me that today
       my friends have been shafted in the rear

       And I spend my weekdays in fear
       of those mobile calls
       from cousins or uncles
       informing me that today
       my family has been shafted in the rear

       And I spend my weekends in fear
       of everything the weekday brings
       from everyone everywhere
       with the capacity to inform me
       that everything will eventually be shafted in the rear

Brongest
There is a plaque here on the pavement where Gracie Fields once split a knee.

Bronington
A laughing five-year-old girl in a pair of dungarees was struggling to string candyfloss into her mouth. She was giggling harder at each of her failed attempts, as a small kitten looked on bemused. I realised someone, somewhere, would see that girl and think: "I would like to have sex with that child." The moment was ruined.

Bronwydd
I am the swill-swallower of next week.

Broughton

Happiness is a little ball of cheese that melts in your underpants, leaving your penis, testicles or vagina slathered in melted cheese, a cheese that cannot be cleaned from your underparts with a brisk genital showering, so that your most intimate regions remain coated in melted cheese for the rest of your cheesy life.

Brymbo

I was chomping on nougat when I recalled the closing scene from Roy Andersson's *A Swedish Love Story*, when a pissed man staggers into a midnight fog, and a screaming horde of friends and family come looking for him. It would be nice to have someone shrieking hysterically at me to please keep on living.

Bryn Offa

"I spit on the residents of Schaan," a spindly man said.

Bryn-y-Baal

Translated, means "Bryn-y-Baal".

Brynamman

The Bergþórusons weaponised cat videos to win the election. Having observed that the world had fallen into two camps: those who watched rage-inducing political videos and those who watched soporific and cute-tastic cat videos, the Icelandic Social Democrats hired the brothers to bag their win. The first camp took their dopamine hits from videos uploaded on amoral media outlets who reaped their revenue from whipping people up into a froth of hatred over immigration. The second hid from this torrential political onslaught in the warm cuddliness of innocent felines. The Bergþórusons created a series of videos of their ministers DESTROYING interlocutors and another series of ministers sitting around petting cats talking about their liberal policies. These appeased the contingent of frothing haters and trolls and the indifferent or afraid swathes of self-obsessed retweeters. It was only during the live television debate, where the ISD candidate sat stroking a calico while DISMANTLING his opponent with fuming rhetoric, where the two sides had their political erogenous zones tingled all the way to the ballot box.

Bryncenydd

Overheard:

"Hello. We met at the *Fresh Writing 28* launch. We were discussing the use of aposiopesis in the texts of Philip Sydney, do you remember? I dared to posit the Foucaultian notion that crypto-normativism was a pre-existing construct dating back to *The Wanderer*, and there was some heated debate about that over the vegan vol-au-vents. I mentioned the study of poetics in the work of Herman Wouk I was working on, and you suggested an agent I could pitch to. I have yet to receive a reply from you. Go suck your mother's cunt."

Bryncethin

If this village was an obscure semi-avant-garde Scottish novelist, it would be Giles Gordon.

Bryncoch

I met a man who workshopped erotica with his mother. "What about the teabagging scene?" he asked her. "Did you ever teabag father?" His mother explained that the woman would not take the man's testicles in her mouth for a whole ten minutes as was written. She explained that the woman would roll her tongue along the bottom of the balls for *at most* under a minute, then move her tongue towards the penis until climax. "What about the anal cleft?" he asked. "Did you ever lick father's anal cleft?" She explained that the female character, if she was to be taken as representing the average woman, would probably not probe the man's anal cleft with her tongue, unless the area had been washed. "What does semen taste like?" he asked. "Did you ever swallow father's semen?" She explained that it was not a characteristic of erotic scenes to concern oneself with the "aftermath", so to speak. That was the prerogative of pornography.

Bryncroes

I tend to nap around 1.30. I wake up headbust and cocklost.

Bryneglwys

This is what the writer Vaughan Grenade said to me:

"I am not writing a second novel. There will be no second novel. There will be no more novels. There will be no more reheated plots and packaged characters. No more microwave thrillers. Boil-in-the-bag romances. No more virtuoso showcases of an MFA-stamped prose in the *Upcoming Whelps Quarterly*. No more workshops with pens being twirled and chins being stroked. No more earnest feedback on lumpen prose and overwrought poems. Fiction on the ooze. Strangers with nine novels in them begging to be expressed. Pastel colours and sunsets and women with blank expressions staring into the middle distance on all book covers until Christendom. There will be no more novels until the backlog is dealt with. The relentless pummelling of transient fictions on a casual readership. The seasonal sainted book and its author retreating to their bucolic nook to pen a forgotten second. The million manuscripts on the desk of A.P. Rose Associates and the two interns skimming them for movie potential. Retired businessmen settling down to pursue literary success. Nineteen-year-old emos self-publishing *The Darkness is Rising III: Darkness Begets Darkness*. There will be no more novels. There will be only apologies. Reader, I am sorry for this novel you are holding in your hands. I simply have no other means of expression and I desperately need an outlet. Reader, maximum apologies! I know this novel does not need to exist. I have toiled at this for three years, so you understand I had to publish? And on the front cover of future bestsellers: YOU DO NOT *NEED* TO READ THIS. HAVE YOU CONSIDERED SOMETHING FROM ANOTHER DECADE? HAVE YOU EVER SPARED A THOUGHT FOR THE AUTHOR WITHOUT MASS COMMERCIAL BACKING, YOU POPULIST WHORE? MIGHT YOU LOOK AT LITERARY TRANSLATIONS? SMALL PRESS BOOKS? MAYBE IF YOU WOULD CEASE FOLLOWING THE HERD FOR THREE MINUTES, YOU MAY DISCOVER A WORLD OF LITERATURE MORE

SUITED TO THE SEMI-INTELLIGENT YOU LURKING SOMEWHERE BELOW? My future, my kingdom for a dream."

Brynford

I shot an elbow with a crossbow.

Bryngwyn

I am in a field, in shoes fuming. I see, in a gormless sheep's face, that look of lemon-mouthed virulence the B&B owner paid me as I entered the premises. I see that look of peanut-throated panic in the owner's teenage daughter as I heaved upstairs. I see that look of bomb-eared mania from the chambermaid as I unlocked the room. I unleash an appropriate salival salvo towards the sheep's face.

Brynhyfryd

"This is only a phase. You will be happy." a man told his son.

"Excuse me," I stepped in. "Depression is natural response when confronted with this bitch of an earth. I speak from painful experience. Get through any way you can, little one. Pills, cheap sex, booze, whatever it takes."

I was punched.

Brynteg

I present, so some accepting assferret might understand, The Quantum Scale of Facial Catastrophes (in five phases):

Quantum Phase I—"The Teenage Girl": You are the sufferer of mild and unnoticeable sebaceous bumps in inconspicuous places—milk spots along your chin, behind your ears, or below your fringe. Essentially, anything that can be easily concealed with a layer of foundation. These unobtrusive, harmless non-pimples, are the sort of thing teenage girls might consider a cause for shrieking self-castigation, the sort of miniscule blemish the Quantum II sufferer considers beneath contempt.

Bryntiron

In Húsavík, men in plaid shirts with rippling chests stride along spotless pavements with their hourglass blonde wives, their smirking faces and faultless skin on show, a high-spirited sprog with Level 3 piano in tow. In Bryntiron, men in soiled cagoules tug their lethargic pitbulls through stinking alleyways, as their plus-size nicotine-mottled wives chain-smoke indoors. I prefer this hellhole to that one.

Burry Port

DREAM [1]: I am living in a shed on Helga's lawn. She occupies a large aristocratic house overlooking the Kollafjörður fjord. She takes exquisite pleasure in pretending my shed and my self is not there.

Burton

'Poem to my 16 Y/O Self' from Barrie Bartmel's *Poems of a Poltroon* (p.6):

> It will come as some relief
> as you prime the video recorder
> to late-night Channel 5
> that sexual intercourse
> is nowhere near as remarkable
> as that thing we do
> under the sheets
> with our right hands
> and our imaginations

Bwlchgwyn

O, Helga... I picture us in the sunlicked silence of a balmy Wednesday, reading short story collections by popular Canadian authors in bed, an hour before the grinding winddown of a long uneventful day, as the cat offers vacant meows in the hallway. I lift my lazy head towards your Munro-moved face, half-opening my mouth in readiness of the words that are never readily speakable...

Bwlchllan
I forgot that I had momentarily lifted my balaclava to pick a pustule, when a small girl looked at me and began screaming. I tried to pretend I was used to that sort of reaction from children. But I still cried.

Bylchau
Overheard: "Mitchell, I hate to tell you this, but you're your own brother."

Cadole
I would commit suicide, if I thought it might upset someone.

Cadoxton
A tall Congolese man arrived at the breakfast bar. The B&B owner, a skittish divorcée with blue-streaked bangs named Fiona Narr, entered with a breakfast salver of croissant, orange pieces, coffee, and two toasts premade for his entrance. "Sleep well? Dormez bien?" she asked. The man nodded and accepted the salver, recoiling when Narr tried to touch his hand while ensuring the victuals were lapped. As she retreated from the room he thought on the frottage that she would perform against his ample buttocks in the cleaning cupboard later, and the invitations to attend rooms in which she would masturbate on a chair to his erect penis, and felt a swell of hopelessness coming over him. (I imagined).

Caeathro
I spotted the writer Vaughan Grenade in a milch bar. He stated:

"Stendhal said 'twenty lines per day, genius or not', and for a spell I adhered to this dictum. Of course, Stendhal never specified the leading of these lines, i.e. whether he was using a notepad with the standard 8.7mm spacing or if he was using Word 2016 or newer, with the automatic double spacing. Stendhal also never specified whether those lines should consist of fiction or text of no fixed topic. In all this panic and confusion, I bought a small notepad and filled twenty lines (about three words per line) with various lists: favourite brands of coffee, least engrossing François Ozon movies, shortest Portuguese novels, thinnest members of girl group The A-Lines, safest brands of moisturiser on the market, and so on. I am still awaiting a publisher for this material. Thanks for nowt, Marie-Henri."

Caer Llan

I was pissed on vodka chasers at Caer Llan House when a blubbering quasi-widow made mouth noises in my right ear. Her husband, an inventor, had vanished two months previous, leaving the introduction to his autobiography folded in the toothbrush holder as his last missive. She handed me a facsimile and asked me to help locate him. As I was already several years or months or whatever through a Wales-wide schlepp, I said sure. In the hotel the next morning I read the opening pages inside a cumulonimbic hangover:

> Hello, Cinnamon.* I am the best Welsh. I invent things and I am a schemer from Gwent. I am known as the "schemer's schemer", first monikered aloud in 1989, and at the mo, I reside in a terracottage in Holyhead with a Balinese mog named Westward Ho! Before I explain what "terracottage" means, I should spend a moment lowering you into my lexical bathysphere, permitting you the necessary time to submerse yourself in the strange waters of my words, to settle into your scuba suit as I pilot you into the sinuously corralled underworld of my face, and the exploits extending therefrom, into the wonderfully fizzy realm of people and things I call "existence".
>
> There. You are lowered.
>
> First, a few words on my paragraphing strategies in this. I am an instinctive paragrapher. I paragraph

---

*Yes, more books should open with addresses to specific readers. The likelihood that someone named Cinnamon is reading this is slim. It is the sort of name the unbrained would slap on their newborn in an attempt to seem alt-kook or nü-weird. However, imagine the pleasure a Cinnamon, having somehow emerged from the sunken ooze of their horrid name, and even more horrid upbringing, will have upon seeing their fore- as the second word in an eminent book. It says to them: "Yes, you too, you too, you too."

along emotional lines, like the poetrymakers, not the London prosesters, with their focus-grouping and scientific measuring of the street-level reader's patience with sentences, who tailor their works to please a phantom metric known as their "audience". No, this is a shenanigan to which I will not boogie. I have so far made a huge concession by not writing in my own English Plus (+++) (later I will introduce you to her sultry lexical ways), or in the form of an illustrated erotic chapbook. My publishers, two Germanic ex-retainers who attended a university, made a persuasive case for me using short to medium-length sentences featuring familiar words that people could mentally parse while eating parsnips and, after two long confrontations with regrettably violent imagery, I conceded. The paragraphs will fluctuate in size, much like a balloon being inflated by an asthmatic kid.

I am the best Welsh. I have lived as a Welsh for five decades. I have schemed and invented more things than the other Welshes, and had more of a secret impact than the louder more extrovert Welsh. This here is my story, unbothered by media sneereries, televisual hohahees, or enemies' slanderringdo. I promise—and I promise unoften as I walk around the skelped promenades of this proud nation—to maintain a level of candour oft-reserved for men at their sunkenest, the beautiful candour of the pre-hanged man in his bunk, nibbling on his last mac and cheese, slurping his last pomegranate and elderflower smoothie, waiting for his state-funded spinal column severance, waxing without a care on the satanic foxtrot he has taken across life's burning coals, as he fixes you with a look that says: "Here, as I end my days in this damp hole, ritually soiling myself in terror, I am for the first time, willing to let the unvarnished truth emerge from my dry, chapped lips, and let you know, yes, *this* is how it was." It is that spirit I will endeavour to channel in the following 1,293 pages.

> I have structured my story across the eight Welsh counties in which I have spent the pivotal moments of my life. It is my intention to croak in Gwent, although I am only 50, so I will probably change my mind and elect to die somewhere nicer.
> — Colin McDonnall, The Best Welsh

Caerau

If this village were a political manoeuvre, it would be Nicolae Ceaușescu's 1980s austerity policy, leading to the murder of babies in Romanian neonatal intensive care units.

Caerfarchell

We made a pledge that if either of us had the chance to screw someone more attractive, we would leap at that chance with gazelle-like gusto. So far, I have had zero chances, Katrin has had around seventeen. As I listen to her screwing a botany student from Aberystwyth Uni, I can't help feeling there is a degree of unfairness to this pledge.

Caergeiliog

I have tried to live a life free from outcast clichés. I have thrust this bubbling boilhead of mine in front of folks and said, "This is my revolting mug. I exist, you assbadgers. I want to do this shit as well. Look at your phone, and text your wibbly girlfriends if I repulse you, you shallow-brained sub-hominid über-fucks."

Caerhun

O, Helga, you have a massive forehead. It must be over fifteen centimetres in width. You have wild unplucked brows. When I return home I will lick that massive forehead and kiss those wild unplucked brows. I will suck on your small pillbox lips as if drawing from Cressida's teat. I will mount you, you raven thing. I will curl you up inside my fortress and snack on you like a Cornish pasty.

Caerphilly

This is what Emmett Coles said to me:

"A few kind words from me, Emmett Coles, premier critic in the *Caerphilly Quarterly*, can make or break a literary career. I exercise this power recklessly, trouncing nubile newbies with their Carverian micronovels, overly ambitious encyclopaedic epics, or homely little novellas about bucolic bust-ups. They come to me, these cherub-faced scribblers, from places as far off as Invergloy, clutching their manuscripts, hoping a few free drinks, flirtatious winks, kindly words muttered into my partially deaf left ear will secure them the Colesian encomium. They must accede to my demands before I scribble so much as a half-clause of praise. My sexual tastes are voracious, so I accept all manner of creatively devised erotic couplings from both sexes, often involving the depilation of poultry. Shakily performed oral underneath the bar table simply will not sate me. Alternatively, I accept public humiliations, such as riding a hog through Ty Castell Guest House while singing numbers from the agit-punk outfit Chumbawumba, or snorting heroin off the baby during a local christening. A full list of "prices" can be found on my Bebo page. Sometimes, even if I have been sated fully by a writer, I will still inexplicably destroy their ambitions because they have irked me in some extremely petty way. They often commit suicide, or send mail bombs through my postbox, but this only spurs me on to be even more arbitrary and vicious in my role as literary editor. Try your best, wannabe writers, because it may get you nowhere, and nowhere in the realm of Emmett Coles is the saintliest position you can ever hope to occupy."

Caewern

Helga, I dreamt that you touched me and the whole planet exploded into a screaming fireball.

Caldicot

I am irritated by all these people on antidepressants and anti-anxiety pills. When will we realise we are allergic to ourselves. We are literally allergic to our own existences, and the pain and dread that we feel every second of every day is like the thrashy sneeze of the hayfever sufferer, or the expletive explosion of the male Tourette. Our lives are an allergy, our mass graves the antihistamine.

Caledfryn

The people here want lime cordial.

Capel Bangor

Translated, means "a snack in the bath that she cannot digest".

Capel Betws Lleucu

From *An Alternative History of Wales*:

201 AD: The Demetae people pioneer the use of water in bathing.

398 AD: Retired Roman leader Magnus Maximus earns £100,000 per annum on the lecture circuit.

879 AD: The kingdom of Deheubarth perceived as smug.

Capel Coch

From the parish Twitter: "I urge that Wilson, the decrepit old never-was, send hostile men with uzis to riddle this useless parish with bullets! Come on, Wilson, how much 'persuasion' is needed? Do I have to resort to sending turds in a bag? First warning."

Capel Colman

I swear I saw the staggered apparition of George C. Scott coming over the hill.

Capel Dewi

This is what Xavier Olman said to me:

"My brother was a bastard child born into a slum. A repulsively ugly baby, George was beaten and mistreated by his scornful parents, never shown an ounce of love or affection. At the age of twelve, George ran away from home, fell in with a crowd of drug addicts and became addicted to heroin. To score, George robbed homes, developing a taste for burglary, grievous bodily harm, and rape. George, having severely beaten nineteen people and raped ten women, was shot in the face by a police officer on his fifteenth birthday."

Capel Garmon

I see: my mother in the mirror, observing me masturbating on the bed, nodding her head as if to say, "well, continue, then!", and my futile attempts to maintain a priapic hunger, and her shaking her head as if to say, "thought not".

Carew Cheriton

Be afraid, Timor-Leste! Icelandic corporate fascism in the warm slippers of liberal democracy is coming!

Carmarthen

"Remember that time your father thought I was a Sephardi Jew, and spat in my crème de menthe?" I asked Katrin.

Carmel

Overheard: "Son, for the last seventy years, I have been sitting on a secret. I must tell you in case my breathing stops. Mitchell, I am actually a palomino horse. I hope you can take it upon yourself to forgive me."

Carnhedryn

Translated, means "we tend to exclude the brown ones".

Carrog

Happiness is a will-o'-the-wisp that vaporises on approach.

Carway

You see, Iceland, your attempts to heal the species with the unguent of smirking liberalism will collide head-on with the snarling idiocy of entrenched bigotry, and you will have to concede that the snug bubble of hate always trumps the well-meaning hug of pretend concern. Give up.

Camp Hill
The Lemonheads are insipid, brain-flattening, twee-bot asshelmets.

Castellan
Helga Horsedóttir, for you, I would scoff as a Sikh curses up a storm on a coach trip to Peebles.

Castlemartin
Björk was unavailable to relaunch Burkina Faso under the new Icelandic rule. Former Sugarcubes bassist and novelist Bragi Ólaffson was sent instead. The citizens of Burkina Faso were "pleased" to have their dictator toppled, though "not as keen" to have their savannas replaced with fjords, the BBC reported.

Cefn Brith
In the rearview mirror, I caught sight of a large pair of buttocks on two thin legs hopping across the wild tufts of farm. I had a hangover and wanted to soak in the tub and read a volume of the Argentine poet Oliverio Girondo, so I let the buttocks continue their hopping business as I pulled into the B&B four miles along the road. Lounging in the tub with a scone, feasting on some sublime Girondoan phrase-making ("My rubber-soled happiness makes me bounce over the sand"), I heard a sequence of seismic thuds. The buttocks, some six-feet up and twelve-feet across, were leaping into the air and arse-plummeting onto sheep. I hasted into a towel and watched the revolting pair of hairless cheeks, bloodied with fur and sheep innards, continue hopping along and targeting static sheep probably already dead from heart attacks, and flattening them under alternating sides. After seven or eight flocculent casualties, a farmer came roaring across the landscape in a 4x4 and leapt from the vehicle with a crossbow. An effective deterrent against rogue elbows, this weapon was not intimidating to the buttocks, which pranced around the man in a taunting cancan as the first bolt missed the left cheek by a whisker. His crossbow, relying on the European rolling nut lock without the usual cylindrical pawl to facilitate easier reloading, failed him as the second bolt

jammed. The buttocks cancanned over to the farmer and released an almighty blast of wind that sent him soaring across the landscape, upward in an elegant farting arc, crash-landing in a marsh that helped break his fall. The buttocks continued their merry sheep massacre, blowing some from time to time similarly to the farmer, their loud impressive farts reverberating across the hollow hills. I was unable to sleep for the sound of these minute-long anal rasps, and the noise of sheep periodically splatting against the B&B ceiling. Fortunately, the police arrived around 3am with a convoy of armed officers, and opened fire on the arse, which twerked off the bullets, until several were aimed into the cleft. An hour later, the cleft began bleeding and the buttocks keeled over dead. The pair were said to have been scientist Armand Godrich, one of the men responsible for the malcogen incident, who had been trapped in a compound and exposed to all sorts of semi-liquid chemical deviltries.

Cefn Coch

This is what A.G. McCulloch said to me:

"Upon starting the laptop, I scan my emails and open Facebook. As I scroll down the wall I observe the image of a drowned child washed up on a beach attached to a petition against the drowning of children, a meme showing close-ups of dogs' noses with the text Dogs Noses Look Like Aliens, Labour contender Jeremy Corbyn's pledge to reverse the arts cuts instigated under the Tories, an article entitled 'Man with almost-perfect poop donates it to help patients with C-diff infection', a click-me vid showing a picture of a 'creeped out' woman that promises to reveal "food marketing's secret weapon", information about the upcoming millionth series of *Doctor Who*, in addition to the usual stream of pictures, uninteresting statuses, online newspaper links, and other reasons to wish to cease communication with each person for whom I once had a fondness. This onslaught of confusing information awaits us each morning and we curb our natural reactions for the sake of politeness. You cannot tell your young cousin that her spelling is atrocious, or your auntie that those pictures of her in provocative undergarments are inappropriate, or that your former colleague's continued successes are strengthening your inferiority complex. I want you to break through this wall of silence. I want you, for a week, to comment honestly on everything on your Facebook wall, regardless of whether your remarks might cause offence. If these people are your real friends, then they can handle whatever you have to tell them, however strong that may seem. This practice will alleviate the angst of having to pretend the bulk of the people you call friends are interesting or amusing. Let me know your results."

"All right," I lied.

Cefn-y-Bedd

If the inside of my head was a noise, and that noise was recorded, and that noise was a 1985 rock masterpiece released through Touch & Go, that noise would be the Butthole Surfers' *Psychic... Powerless... Another Man's Sac.*

Cefnmeriadog

I took to naming my blemishes after members of influential shoegazing bands. I had a particular fondness for Bilinda Butcher (#12), Emma Anderson (#6), and Rachael Goswell (#19).

Chapel of Ease

I see: my father kissing my mother on the nose, and my mother's unconvincing receipt.

Churchill Park

Katrin: "My auntie said to me, 'I am afraid Satan dwells within your pelvis. At some point, we will have to pipette God's love through your ureter and kill the evil that lurks in your urinary glands.'"

Chwilog

"We're bedraggled, harassed, bodily boxed, and seriously duffed up because from birth we are forced to achieve more than our feeble brains and bodies can possibly handle. If we make limping through every day without embarrassing ourselves the one parameter of success, the thing might be easier," Katrin said.

Cilgerran
Barrie Bartmel proved that martyrdom is the way forward for poets. One volume, one miserable suicide. You can't have it both ways, poets: success and being alive.

Cimla
Nothing on this planet is worth fighting for. I am surprised we have lasted this long.

Clarbeston
"I utterly loathe you this morning," I said.

"Why?" Katrin asked.

"Dunno. I look at you and I loathe everything about you. Not merely your externals—your blotchy face, or your paunchy little stomach—but your lack of ideals and complete surrender to self-loathing hedonism."

"Oh. I have no particular feelings either way about you."

Clawdd Coch
I urinated on the grave of Betty Evans, b.1899, d.1946. Nothing personal.

Clunderwen
I met a Scottish man who explained his loathing of crime novelist Ian Rankin to me.

"I was whelped, without a wisp of conference, in a poor wet nation named Scotland. In this poor wet nation we have four main means of rustling up rupees to fatten Lady Earth's coffers. The first is letting small rooms and cupboards from which assorted Londoners and Americans can stare awestricken at lochs. The second is selling unpleasant malt beverages for people to sup while staring awestricken at lochs. The third is letting undersize plastic chairs from which persons can squint toward millionaires booting a leather bag around fake grass for an hour over the promised running time. The fourth is the rendering into prose of sex crimes, stabbings, shootings, and smotherings in perpetually Novemberish cities: the crime novel. There are around 30+ successful Scottish crime novelists, and 3500+ unsuccessful or unpublished ones. These writers, tirelessly prolific, seemingly unstoppable, clack their creations into being at the rate or two or three novels per annum. Their protagonists are cop ciphers who solve evil stuff—an endless smörg of asphyxiations, buggerings, chokings, maimings, throat-slashings, and the occasional Fiat Uno theft. These writers bring income to publishers, because these writers have readers. And in creative writing classes spanning the Mull of Galloway to Oosta, sit clumps of aspiring crime writers with their procedurals set in local towns and conurbs, featuring more beleaguered malt-tanking puzzle-solving philandering perma-divorced sneer-lipped hard-talking DIs and DCs than the land's actual police stations (where the staff spend 70% of their time in conference rooms with crime novelists). And the unofficial king among these lovers of murder and sex crimes is the fecund imp Ian James Rankin OBE," he said.

"All right. Stop there. 'Lovers of sex crimes'?"

"Quote me correctly," he insisted.

"Fine, 'lovers of [. . .] sex crimes'."

"Better."

"Stranger," I patronised, "your middle name is 'sad parsnip'. These writers are smart for having identified the audience's lust for rapes, stabbings, slashings, and other shrieks of vicarious misanthropy, and finding a form for exacting their own revenge fantasies. And one, I must add, that yields monthly yen, that drums up monthly deutschmarks, that poops out monthly pfennigs, that zaps monthly zlotys, that . . ."

"Enough."

"These writers have tapped into what Zola called 'the beast in man', i.e. our lust for seeing someone's skull crushed like a pomegranate under a steamroller, our lust for seeing someone richer, sexier, funnier, eviller, nicer, or literally anyone who isn't us, have their brains rearranged into Rorschachs across the wainscoting. If you could make thousands of monthly kwacha exploiting these truths, you would."

"I can address this piffle. Yes, a clever means of misanthropic succour. But these embittered writers have let their insane loathing for humankind bleed into the publishing world with their unapologetic milking of the brand. For every fifteenth installment in the DCI Robulus series, a more imaginative and competent novel from an unknown writer is mouldering on a to-read pile, while the publisher proofreads another scene of a barman having his right knee knived in a Possil pub. These crime hacks have monopolised the Scottish publishing machine, smothering the realm of infinite invention ("literature") under reams of uninspired workmanlike prose. And those writers currently at the teat on MA programmes at fine Scottish universities will have nowhere to publish their alt-kook and nü-weird works, have no one to whisper the words 'promising' or 'up-and-coming' into their ears . . . what will the next crop of novelists resemble? The macerated corpse on p.272 that constitutes 'the twist'. My friend, no need to be upset. All I am saying is that these crime novelists have perpetuated the biggest and most heinous crime of all: strangling the future of Scottish literature."

"It was a strain to meet you."

"I haven't finished."

"Diddums."

Clydach

I met an insane man in aquamarine clodhoppers clad in the flag of the former Soviet Republic.

"But I digress," he said. "How can I digress when I haven't started yet? I digress from not starting into starting. But I digress from this explanation. Surely this isn't *digression* but *progression* as per the movement of narratives? But I digress from this question. How can I digress when the question hasn't been answered yet, you might ask? But I digress from this . . . I forget what it is I'm digressing from. But I digress from this short-term memory loss. I am a pathological digresser. But

I digress from this confession. I can't stop digressing from my digressions. But I digress . . . from what? The doctor suggested I take these new anti-digression pills for my problem. But I digress from this prescription. I'll take one now. But I digress from this pill-popping. What happens when I take my anti-digression pills is that I . . . trail off and forget what it was I was . . . things. It's not a form of digression . . . worse because I can't even complete a whole sentence without . . . it's better at least being able . . . with the digressions. Even more vexing . . . work and places like that is . . . I get tired and end up . . . "

(I met no such man).

Clydach Vale
If Cerberus was neutered, brought strenuously to heel with a cat-o'-nine-tails, shampooed and vacuumed for a twelve-year stint inside the perfumed room of a Barbara Cartland-obsessed spinster, and fed exclusively on a diet of vegan meat chunks and soya milk, you would have the Bergþóruson brothers.

Clynnog Fawr
Nowhere in the world have I seen a canonical sundial this resplendent.

Coed Eva
Yes, I posted two thousand words of bile on an Arianda Grande forum.

Coedana
I see: the terror in Katrin's face whenever her mobile chirrups.

Coedcanlas
This is what Isadora Pledge said to me:

"I introduced foods into the bedroom for extra sexual pizzazz with luscious Loretta (a craven little minx from Maiden Wells with a nine-mile tongue). At first, she was turned on at the sensual potential of this notion, but when I brought through butter, Marmite, and chicken soup she formed a face of unsexy perplexment. She had imagined more prosaic nibbles like strawberries or chocolate buttons in this scenario, not entire brunches. As I was turned on at the prospect of smearing Loretta's tum in Marmite and flooding her breasts in chicken soup, our sexual sesh reached a stalemate. In time—well, with a little lover's pleading—Loretta consented to have her tum smeared in Marmite if it fired me up, but I could read the repulsion on her phiz. She was wondering what sort of industrial-strength soap she would need after to unyield the yeast extract. I never fucked Loretta much after that."

Coedpoeth
You are primed to pop on Christmas morn, Adam Franklin.

Coity
You have to admire Arab Strap for turning 2AM puke-mouthed pub-floor ramblings into a viable art form.

Colwinston
Recalling my first kiss with Katrin, in a stranger's brown shed somewhere in Laugarbakki circa Nov 2011, I picture the opening scene of Jens Lien's *The Bothersome Man*, where an affectless couple in an affectless bourgeois dystopia snog with all the tongue-slavering affectlessness of two depressed prepubescents.

Cribyn
You see, Iceland, the history of humankind is a mountainous monument to frothing spitting hatred. Our species is hard-wired to set itself on fire with spectacularly expensive production values. It is our biggest talent.

Crick
When we say "I hate you", we are really saying "I cannot love you, since years of parental and societal contempt have hardened me forever towards any naïve notions of love or compassion. However, this warped inversion of love is the closest thing we will ever have to love, so we should pretend to find solace in it."

Crickhowell

My heart is non-aurous. It is a lump of plutonium in the yawning mouth of a newborn kitten.

Croes Hywel

I contest that happiness is impossible, for our memories are working constantly to undercut our pleasures with reminders of the rancidity of things. Moments that seem uncontestably mirthful only have a limited window before some mental carnage arrives to utterly poleaxe your moments of reprieve. It is the cutting of counterbalance. For instance, you might be sitting there in your cotton socks, lapping up a bowl of steaming custard. Then you remember that man in Bucharest who punched your wife in the eye. Your pleasure decreases. You try to resume your custard unbothered. Then you remember the men who lied to your sister about the safety of electrolysis as a cure for headaches. Your pleasure decrements. You remember that child who borrowed your strimmer to murder a weevil. It decrements. It is a programmable phenomenon. If we take shrieking right-wing skeleton Anne Coulter as our variable, we can compute this decremental cognitive assault effect on our happiness:

```
if (x == 'annecoulter') {
    for (i=0; i<100; i--) {
        pleasure--;
    }
}
```

Croesor

DREAM [35]: A tall man who has penetrated Helga over seventy times shows me the lustre of his semi-erect penis from the bay window, fresh from his seventy-third penetration.

Croespenmaen

155,000,000 Pot Noodles per annum.

Crogen

The reason the nanonation of Liechtenstein chose to bombard the county borough of Flintshire with a merciless hail of exploding things is still unclear. The most convincing explanation is that a local Flintshire councillor had heard a rumour that coal abounded in the region and paid a corrupt Liechtensteinian official to sanction an airstrike that the PR machine would spin as a "weapons test failure" (as it was then reported in the world media) in order to check whether there was a rich seam of that natural resource below. Another explanation is that a Welshman with a weak bladder from Flintshire on a castle tour of Austria and Liechtenstein had experienced a series of unfortunate mishaps, first urinating on the floor of the Burg Gutenberg castle, then against the Obere Burg walls, then from a helicopter onto the keep of Vaduz Castle, and then on an antique Gothic Revival chair in Liechtenstein Castle, Lower Austria. Taken as a pointed attack on the heritage of the nation, an airstrike was launched at the incontinent man's house in Flint to blow him from the planet (the first bomb landed on Duke Street, on orders from the Duke of Urach, owner of Liechtenstein Castle).

Cross Hands

There is a plaque here on the statue Elkie Brookes once cropped out of a photo.

Crosswell

The problem with the later works of Émile Zola is their interminable, flatulent preachiness.

Crugybar

I am the swollen neck of the body politic.

Crundale

People tell me this place burst into song once in 1923.

Crunwere

DREAM [20]: Half a walnut in my wicked crooks. The taste of your hair in my soup.

Crynant

I swear I saw the staggered apparition of William G. Stewart coming over the hill.

Cwm

You might wonder, Bergþórusons, what compels me to complete this Cambrian odyssey, when most people would have lost their mind in Llandudno. I refuse to allow you to sack me for failure to complete this mission. I want you, upon completion, to have to read, or pay some minion to read, every word of these "reports", and I look forward to the looks on your faces when I return with my completed document, and the panic that you will now have no reason to action my riddance, what with my having completed one of the most thorough and ridiculous expeditions in the Institute's history. Yes, Bergþórusons, this is spite—beautiful, uncomplicated spite—at your lavish expense.

Cwmafan

Overheard:

"At the advice of Simon Drainage, I have decided to contradict what I wrote in the last paragraph and open the tale with a short description of the man who will purchase the loaf. The man, Gerald Harold Horseman, occupied a small cottage in the hamlet of Poke in North Area. Born into an industrious working class family, Gerald's father rose up from his origins to manage a sawmill and his mother became a respected GP, allowing Gerald the privilege of comfort and the freedom to choose his occupational fate from a well-heated and large bedroom. As is often the case with the children of the nouveau riche, Gerald lacked the motivation to succeed in one selected field and spent his twenties living in a parent-funded flat in Poke, hanging around the bars and clubs, having meaningless sexual encounters with equally wayward women that led to mutually emotionally unsatisfying relationships lasting three or four months at most. This behaviour continued until he found himself approaching thirty, having never held down an occupation in his life. At some point before his thirtieth birthday, Gerald checked the cupboards and noticed he was running low on bread."

Cwmbach
I licked a dead elbow for the lols.

Cwmbran
I am bawling in a bowling alley lav. There's a watermelon in my lap.

Cwmbrwyno
This is what Martin Cohen said to me:

"Martin Cohen—that's I—had tender nubbins. The location of these nubbins, the precise nature of the nubbins' tenderness, and the preferred Oxford definition of the term 'nubbins' in a medical or otherwise context, was never made clear to the others. The principal fact about Martin Cohen was that he suffered from tender nubbins, and efforts to prise specifics from the secretive lips of the man were fraught with sensitive outbursts and epic sulks. No one who had seen Martin in the nude, either old school friends or past lovers, was locatable, because Martin had taken steps to encrypt his past through conflicting information passed to various people in confidence, in public, and on the internet. There was the Martin Cohen born to two teenage parents in passenger seat of a Renault Espace, the Martin Cohen born on a windless hillock to a single mother in the satellite dish repair trade, the Martin Cohen born in the stalls during an Alexei Sayle performance at the Dragon Club, and innumerable Martin Cohens born to single mothers and loving couples in numerous specified and unspecified locations, the one unchanging truth being the newborn's name: Martin Cohen. Apart from this, nothing about Martin Cohen—that's I—was remarkable, and in appearance he resembled the long-serving bassist of The Fall, Steve Hanley, circa 1982, after the release of the *Hex Enduction Hour* LP."

Cwmcarn

The surrealism in Beck's oeuvre might be read as an attempted artistic evacuation of scientological principles, hard-coded across a childhood of conditioning.

Cwmcarvan

DREAM [17]: I have two overnight pails. One pail catches rain from the ceiling and the other my tears shed from watching tall men hold Helga. In the morning I cannot tell which is which.

Cwmfelinfach

I am the noxious corner of chance.

Cwmisfael

Bergþórusons, once this is over, I will spend the rest of my days undermining your attempts to heal the world with ecoffee cups, bekittened snoods, and the novels of Dave Eggers.

Cwmparc

I imagined in italics the items inside Helga's livingroom . . . *a leatherette sofa with a pre-fingered copy of* Classic Rock Today *featuring a candid interview with The Edge and a track-by-track analysis of 2 Unlimited's upcoming album; a cushion with a hand-embroidered tableau of an earless rabbit perched in a either a pool of urine or melted daffodils; a half-drunk plastic bottle of pineappleade; a maroon cigarette lighter with a falcon emblem atop a copy of Lermontov's* A Hero of Our Time; *an uncreased letter from the mortgage company Valcheck & Co outlining their various concerns with the current situation; a cerise-coloured carpet with a prominent stain from a black coffee knocked from the sofa and blotted in an erroneous panic into the shag; a copy of the lyric sheet to The Beautiful South's* Welcome *with the tense error in 'Have You Ever Been Away?' underlined; a clutch of unopened letters in toast rack on the mantlepiece; a bag of nails on an empty ottoman; a flatpack crib boxed and unassembled in the corner below an abstract painting from artist Snell Greedlee of seven concentric circles terrorised by a splat of eggshell; a pair of coloured tights on an unwashed plate with remnants of broccoli and swede; an air freshener broadcasting the scent of 'Misty Hillocks'; an incomplete handwritten letter to 'Dennis', calling for some form of reciprocal emotional response; a TV remote with the 'mute' button pressed too far in to function; a leprechaun figurine mounting a Highland cow figurine in a terracotta pot . . .*

Cwmpennar
I am lapping at stout when I recall the scene from Ruben Östlund's *Play*, when a frightened child scurries up a tree to avoid a mugging from a series of older boys. I always believed that courage is another form of cowardice.

Cwmsychbant
"I really want to spit in your filthy, hideous face," Katrin said to me over a plate of egg. Sometimes I question the parameters of my self-loathing.

Cwmtillery
Translated, means "a stupid amount of nectar".

Cwmynyscoy
I am in a paradoxical clench. My years as an outcast have left me with an unbending cynicism for the 4/4 rhythms of life, yet I long to nestle into the hessian-stitched arms of Helga Horsedóttir, and raise two pockfacedly cutesy nippers from an ice-blue thatched cottage overseeing the lugubrious thaw of the Tjörnin. How could I survive in the straight world after so long askew in the bent?

Cwmyoy
Translated, means "beanbaggèd man in a weird embrace".

Cwrtnewydd
Katrin: "Last time we screwed, I pictured you as former Bayern Munich captain Oliver Kahn. What was that about?"

Cyfarthfa

One time, a sweet-shanked prostitute talked me into removing the balaclava. She told me that she had slept with wheelchairers, wrinklies, and waistbanderers, and that I would pose no threat. That the misshapen should not be treated as outcasts, and that all bodies are beautiful, and other Facebook memes that hold no stock in the wan light of the real. I removed the balaclava. She snapped back with a repulsed wince. I ran to the toilet and screamed at her to leave the fuck at once. It was a Brobdingnagian slap. I seriously contest that that whore wounded me more in that moment than a lifetime of snide remarks.

Cyffylliog

If this place were a parametric curve, it would be a Bézier with the coefficients of a convex hull.

Cymmer

Helga Horsedóttir, for you, I would remind a neglectful chemist that he left his bifocals on the sideboard.

Dafen

"Hang in there!" a man told his son.

"Excuse me," I stepped in. "This is parent-speak for 'You will never amount to much. Your below-par intellect and lack of awareness about the fixed destinies awaiting to choke your entire adult life renders my teaching pointless.' "

I was not punched.

Dale

Helga Horsedóttir, for you, I would kiss a tot with whooping cough to help fight respiratory gremlins.

Deeside

There is a plaque here outside the pub where Simon Hoggart once ordered a Belgian stout.

Deiniolen

I am writing a TV pilot featuring the things that are omitted from most TV shows. The script is half an hour of men and women belching and farting and lolling around unshaven without makeup caked in sweat and semen.

Deri

"You want to hear how a mate of mine ended up in the sewer?" a pub random asked.

"Nope," I said. I was in a black mood. The horizon was a planet of burning ash.

"Go on. It won't take long."

"Fine," I said. He tabulated his tale.

> In a semi-thatched cottage near a puddle, Morag Evans served baked beans to a man. An unshaven Welsh in a beige cardigan was the recipient of these beans, tipped from a steaming pot onto two slices of unburnt toast. He sat in silence as the beans in their tomato lagoon sopped the toast, replacing crunchiness with sponginess, breaching their borders onto the plate's corners. This rising mound of steaming beans, having long exceeded a sensible toast-topping amount, was an expression of Morag's tetchiness, stemming from a remark made nine hours prior around the time of cereal.
>
> The man, Caradoc McCluster, was used to improper portions as a means to extract a festering sore from their morning blather, and continued to appear unbothered. It had started in March 2013, at the tailend of their romancing period, when Caradoc made his first criticism, commenting on the skimpiness of Morag's portions, and watched her blissful smile wilt to a repulsed rictus. He observed the four pots on heat and braced himself for an onslaught of beans, piling up and slopping around his plate, long surpassing the volume his stomach might process without rectal blowback. He was keen to refuse this legu-

minous invitation to a barney on PJ Harvey's *White Chalk*, the cause of that morning's peevedness, and spooned the steaming beans into his mouth after vigorous cooling blows.

Morag had been fingering the latest news on the flooding outside Port Talbot and munching on natural wheatgerm as *White Chalk* took the room. Caradoc, still in that postconscious bumble when the freedom of expression in one's sleeping interactions and the self-censoring one requires for living when awake with other human beings were still awaiting the brain's untanglement, said: "That's a tad wristslitty for 7.48AM." This remark sent an ugh of irritation up her spine. She was luxuriating in the haunting pianos and zithers, in these beautiful songs hewn from the history of female suffering, stark cries from a bleak and oppressive past. To have this art smudged with a facetious coinage—she could feel his satisfaction with *wristslitty*, how very Joycean—was to take the next eight hours and prick them with pinpricks. Across the Tuesday, she brooded on this snide aside, the flip brainlessness of the remark from the lips of a Welsh oaf. He seemed to suggest that melancholic art needed some proper time and place to be appreciated, or that there was a link between a song's tone and one's mood. These assertions were untested mush from a mouth pulling up words from the posterior. She let her irritation simmer, using that night's bean excess as her means of release.

He spooned in the beans with swiftness, his half-second blows insufficient coolers. His mouth was burning. He fingered the news: a blind Gwynedd man had stabbed a puppy by mistake, a surgeon had sewn a SIM card into someone's sternum. He faked unfazedness as the bean mound reached munro status. It was apparent that the source of her anger was substantial as she unlidded the third pot of beans, three-fourths full, and commenced tipping. It was now impossible to prevent overspill. The plate's curved edges had hampered such an episode so far: now the bean levee had broken. Morag knew, with her four pots of steaming Heinz containing five tins per pot, that she would extract the question from Caradoc's charred lips. If he wanted the relentless, inevitable onslaught of steaming beans to cease, and the burning to stop, he would ask that simple question. If he wanted the beans, creeping towards the table's edge, en route to his trousers, to stop, he knew the question. If he wanted the beans, slopping their tomato selves onto his crotch and lap to stop, he knew the question.

"What's up?" he surrendered. Erin paused her pouring.

"Your flip criticism of *White Chalk* this morning stank like two skunk eggs," she said.

"It wasn't a criticism."

"You insinuated that melancholic music was not appropriate for breakfast listening. That our delicate ears and tenuous mental states might be sent into a spasm upon hearing minor chords. That there was some pre-required timeslot for such wristslittilicious music to be appreciated. What time is that, exactly?"

"I made no such insinuations."

"Then outline your evident beef with this disc."

"Fine. If you have to know, and I know you really have to know, or your world as we know it will come crashing to earth with a splatty thud, the record is the sort of self-absorbed asswank common to indie luvvies no longer concerned with pleasing the listener. Harvey has become the kind of outlier artist who takes half a decade between albums and exploits her fans' willingness to follow her into experimental nooks and noodling crannies. In this, she jettisons listenability for artistic indulgence. This whole album has an ice-hearted tone of mirthless misery, a shameless writhing in bottomless boohoo. There is nothing here except the stink of artistic arrogance and critic-baiting."

"As usual, your understanding is superficial. Having capitulated to commercial pressures with the *Stories From the City* LP, she pursued a unique path that set her apart from most female rockers of the period. She appreciates that her listeners admire her risks and adventures, and these intelligent ears are willing to follow her into the cavernous recesses of this Hardyean dolour. The songs on this record are absolutely breathtaking—in the literal sense of sucking the breath from you with their lonely aura."

"I prefer *Rid of Me*."

"Right, come on."

"What are you doing?"

"Come on."

Morag moved Caradoc from his hot-trousered slump to the bathroom. Uneaten beans in their tomato slime slimed across the carpet. She flipped up the toilet seat and brute-pushed him into the bowl so his feet wedged into the u-bend entrance. A similar punishment had been meted out in the past, when she prodded him into a cold bath packed with ice cubes, after which she felt big contrition and provided nineteen kisses. He waited for her mania to subside, as it had in the past. As she was stood on the sink whacking him on the head with a mop, however, like some bellicose preteen whack-a-moling the mole, this seemed less probable on this occasion. Having crammed his lower legs further into the bowl, she leapt off the sink and clamped him in her strong boxercised arms, using a mixture of mop-whacking and hard vicious shoving to complete her action. Caradoc released a stream of swears and howls in resistance, clawing the bathroom towel on the door to help prevent the descent. Once his legs were secure, it was a matter of force, and she beat his torso into the porcelain depths.

His incredulous, frothing head remained sticking from the u-bend entrance, and she took a moment to pap the image on her phone before combining her final whack with a flush. Caradoc went whooshing up and along and down the pipe, left to the mercy of the North Wales plumbing network.

He vanished into the sewer. The spectacular concatenation of pipes that constituted the North Welsh subterranean plumbing network, in concert with the Port Talbot water authority, spat him into a sewer two miles south of Goytre. He unpacked his aching limbs, wiped the excrement from his sodden skin, and squinted into the torch light of a phone. A line of men were sat on a pipe smoking roaches and talking roaches.

"I wish I could return to a time when I forgot roaches exist," one said, toking the roach. A voice was hurled in Caradoc's area.

"You been flushed?"

"Isn't that apparent?" he replied. His limbs made clicking sounds like secured seatbelts.

"A sarcastic one, here! We've been flushed too, pal. We're having a toke and a talk. You wanna hit o' the roach?" one man offered. He appeared to outstretch an effluential mitt with a proffered bong.

"No thanks," Caradoc said.

"Hang fifteen, man! Fella's two seconds out the pipe and you're trying to turn him pothead. You wanna sewer shot?" Another one appeared to offer an alcoholic beverage in a shot glass.

"What's the shit content?"

"0% shit content, brother."

"Thanks," he said, taking the shot and swigging hard.

The huddle of flushed males came into focus. The shard of light from whoever's phone, resting now on the pipe, showed a foursome of unshaven miscellaneous scruffs of similar vintage and body odour to himself.

"Your first flushing?" one asked.

"Yeah."

"Relax. We're a welcoming bunch in this here sewer. This is Michael Lament. This is David Yoke. This is Neil Souse. I'm Oliver Billingsgate," Oliver said, having pointed to the mentioned people in his hello. "You?"

"Caradoc McCluster. My girlfriend flushed me for criticising PJ Harvey's 2008 LP *White Chalk*."

"Oooffftttt!" David said.

"Hohoho!" Oliver said.

"Shitsticks and prawn sandwiches, mate!" Neil said.

"Pisstractors and shitgiblets!" Michael said.

"One of those challenging feminist albums," David added. "The women love how that shrieking and reverb dredges up the doomed heroines of Victorian fiction. The male critics roll over and praise the album's courage, for fear of reprisals. It is an *important* album. Is it something that the average fan would spin a second time? Nope. I posit that your woman—pardon my socks, mate, what's her moniker?"

"Morag Evans."

"I posit that Morag Evans spun that record from a sense of artistic respect. I bet that morning her ears were calling out for a spin of *Let England Shake*—a record that marries bleakness to actual melodies—or for the charms of *Is This Desire?* But she realised she hadn't spun *White Chalk* twice, and wanted to show she respected PJ's intense vision from a sense of feminine cohortitude. What track was she on?"

"I couldn't say, David."

"I posit that it was track two or three. Did she continue to listen to the album once the criticism was lodged in her aurals?"

"No, she switched it off in a huff."

"Bolívar! Yes! There we have the nub. She used that criticism as an incentive to kill the record."

"You know, that makes a heap of sense."
"Doesn't it?"
He crushed the roach and a passing roach underfoot to underline the success of his impromptu reasoning. A moment's silence passed for the impressiveness of the argument until Caradoc coughed up a tampon.

"You aren't the most concise of storytellers, are you?" I asked.
"Haha," he hahaed.
"I hadn't intended that as a friendly criticism."
"Noted. Anyway, onwards with our tale."

"When is the thatching scheduled for completion?" Linda asked.
"It's one of those things there's never a right time for, like taking last year's Christmas tree to the tip, or reading an Iris Murdoch novel," Morag said.
"Or noting the wit of Suggs."
"Or baking a malt loaf."
"Or telling your father his nose hair is repelling strangers."
"Exactly. So, I flushed Caradoc. Thanks for coming round, babe. I needed you tonight," Morag said. Linda was the friend with a conical head whose counsel she sought on the innumerous occasions she had occasion to boot Caradoc from her semi-thatched cottage, following a wrathful war of words. Linda had been burned in love to Fawkes-strength levels of explosive burniness, and relished the ever-closer prospect of seeing Caradoc kicked to the kerb for his arseholeries, although she had the nagging problem of pathological reasonableness and outstanding conciliation abilities that snuffed the prospect and led to a 100% reunion rate between the uncoupled couple.
"There is a point there, Lindie," she said with her reasonable hat on. "I mean, whatever the stylistic brilliance,

or boldness of a particular piece of art, the success behind a polarising work is whether the audience wants to consume it more than once. In the case of a novel or a film, one reading or viewing is all the creator expects. A musician, unless a composer of long intricate suites, writes songs that ask for a second hearing. The songs on *White Chalk* are not up there on most people's Harvey listen-lists. You have admit that you reached for that album from a sense of obligation. The same sense of obligation the consumer has in sitting through *12 Years a Slave* or *The Act of Killing*. You know the trauma is coming hard and soon and the sweeping horror is about to hit your heart with the force of a battering ram. You would rather be watching something with Emma Thompson. You would rather be listening to *Stories From the City, Stories From the Sea*. If you were honest with yourself."

"As usual, you burrow into the muck of the matter in under twelve minutes of arrival."

"That's me," Linda said, fixing her fringe to make her head appear less conical.

"My God. Can we wrap this up? I can't stand the sound of your voice," I said.

"Fine! My Lord, you are an impatient droog. Here's a truncated ending."

Having toked and supped for nineteen minutes—the question of where the sewer men had sourced their cigarettes and alcohol hanging unsaid in the air like an unwanted high-five from a moron—the fivesome advanced. The men made a slow wade through the long strip of sodden faeces that was the North Wales plumbing network until an exit presented itself in the form of a shaft of light and a climbing ladder. The lads went upwards and arrived in the backcusp of Port Talbot in a place that means 'Dead Meat' in Welsh patois. Meanwhile, Morag went cruising with Linda to look for the nearest sewer entrances and exits, calling "Carrie!" while tanking rums and cokes. They had tippled for an hour before, and continued necking with impunity, stumbling across the pavements and roads in a most uncouth manner. Caradoc found them shrieking "Carrrrie!" in a ditch. He left Linda to pass out and carried his lover in his arms back to the cottage, where he put her to bed after removing her mud-caked clothes. He tried to rouse her for sex, but she was too zonked. In the morning nothing was said. The end.

"Thanks for wasting an hour of my life, you verbose, rambling, styleless windbag from Hades," I said.
"Y'welcome. Another pint?"

Derwyn
I had two choices. I could retreat into hermit-like obscurity, sealing myself up in a basement room like a cut-price Kasper Hauser, viewing the shoes of life squelching along the pavement from my mud-caked porthole, taking short hooded excursions for medical purposes; or I could impose this sebaceous pothole of a face on the populace with flamboyant hostility, matching their violent revulsion with unstinting persistence, never for a second soliciting sympathy. I chose the latter. There is nothing worse than the loveable, self-apologetic cripple. We are not dutybound to make you feel comfortable.

Devauden
Mother: "A sow in hog's clothing is still a big fat oinking pig."

Dihewyd
You are a small ball of pus. You live inside one of my pustules, probably Andrew Sheriff. You have been slowly churning your bacteria and serum, pondering the proper moment to launch yourself into the light to cause maximum pain to my face. You observe, from a sneaky chink in your opaque sac that a straggle-haired beauty from Vík is talking to me and chuckling at my witty observation that Baltasar Kormákur's

101 Reykjavík is a slab of cynical neo-hipster indie. You choose the exact moment she is poised to surrender her phone number, the exact moment she is poised to overlook your wild pimpliness in favour of your quality of wit, the exact moment she is poised to welcome you into the warm embrace of sensuality and lust, you choose that exact moment to explode from your sac with a sinful spurt of runny rheum, launching your yellowy bacterial slime into my longing love-starved lips. You motherfucking Teut. Your act of vengeful sabotage, you heartless ball, has murdered my one shot at love.

Dinas Dinlle
A hollow sensation. The sea.

Dolgarrog
Sometimes I worry when I am forking spaghetti into my maw that I think precisely nothing for weeks on end.

Dolmelinllyn
"Sometimes when we're screwing I imagine inserting a screwdriver up your anus," Katrin said.

Dolwyddelan
I receive a card every Valentine's Day from my mother, with a picture of a heart inside a 'no entry' sign and the caption below: "Remember, no one will ever love you." No matter where I am in the world, this card always seems to reach me, like a light-hearted parental cudgelling in the face. She claims that the card is intended to keep me facing cold hard reality, and rescue me from the futile and time-sucking pain of pining for women who will never fuck me. She might have a point and I hate her.

Downing
I would like to purchase a coffee that shows in the foam the haggard and defeated expression I wear at having capitulated to the chokehold of cutthroat capitalism without the merest yelp of protest.

Drefach

Helga, here are five things I would do to secure a flecklet of your ardour:
1. Talk up the virtues of Right Said Fred to a Crip.
2. Divebomb naked into a croc-dense swamp.
3. Rate each crisp in order of saltiness, flavour, adherence to their advertised shape, and bulkiness in the bag.
4. Listen to Dylan's *Down in the Groove* on a loop for seven hours.
5. Crawl into a damp crevice.

Drope

Have I been?

Drury

There is no point in pretending. Gallic post-rock outfit Call Me Loretta should have been bigger.

Dryslwyn

I met Katrin the eighth time in a Greek restaurant. Over a bowl of moussaka, she told me that her father was flatulent and aloof.

Dulas

Sorry, Miki Berenyi, I had to burst you.

Dwygyfylchi

'Fear' from Barrie Bartmel's *Poems of a Poltroon* (p.30):

    fear of change
    fear of change
    fear of change
    fear of change
    fear of change
    fear of change
    fear of change
    fear of change
    fear of change
    fear of change

fear of change
fear of change
fear of change

Dylife
It was late. I had necked seven whiskies and a limeade chaser. In a haze of burp, I recalled in italics the horror of being born . . . *your first human contact the rubbered hands of a yawning locum who without permission snips your half of the umbilical cord; the wan overhead lighting in the room bringing no real sense of theatre to the occasion; the realisation after five seconds that you have been forced into existence with no prior consultation and that your mother is a selfish and uncaring asshole you instantly loathe; the notable lack of oohs and aahs in the room indicating you are either hideously formed or that very few people care you are now here; your mother's failure to overcome her own exasperation to fake a pleased smile now that you are swaddled in her sweaty arms; your fondness for the layer of amniotic fluid and blood that will never henceforth sheen upon on your skin; the sheer torture of no longer being safely encased in a heavenly womb where your room and board is provided free of charge; worrying that you might have to present your National Insurance Number to the locum when you haven't the capacity to read letters or numbers yet; not being told about Tom Waits so assuming everyone everywhere and everything everyplace is completely pointless; the smug look of an unidentified relative that says 'I can play hopscotch like a boss, and you are a mewling bundle of goo'; your mother's face clearly worrying that you will turn into a pathetic failure and lifelong financial burden and that she should have signed up to that zoology course instead; the six minutes that have elapsed in which the father has failed to present himself; the concern that crying loudly is your natural state, and that you might be crying loudly for the rest of your life; that surge of suicidal panic when your arms desperately reach for the snipped umbilical cord so you can swiftly hang yourself . . .*

Dyserth
Sometimes the afternoon trickles with uncompromising exactitude into a bog.

Earlswood

"I sex up media in the East Wales area. I use manipulative images to entice users into clicking on content. If you wanted to be unkind, you might call me a clickbait artist. For example, say I want to yoke a reader into looking at how they might save £500 on their insurance premium. I deploy a picture of a young lady with large breasts. Or, if I want to show how an old man managed to escape a gang of robbers, I deploy a picture of a young lady with large breasts. This is my profession. I am a leader in my field," Timothy Hall said to me.

East Williamston

There is a plaque here outside the shop where Bob Holness once bought a colander.

Edern

My mother mistook the waspish cynicism of a bourgeois feminist for a solid foundation of unconditional love and support. It happens.

Edwinsford

"I spit on your crime-free carelessness," a spindly man said.

Eglwyswrw

The people here want a form of proportional representation where a proper cross-section of political ideologies have a broader impact across the nation. (Kidding! The people here want to clamp Romanians).

Elan Village

If this village was lacking a particular concept, that particular concept would be élan.

Elliotstown

Katrin: "My auntie said to me, 'The road you hoe is the road to Hell. We have tried poultices, leeches, and an exorcism, and nothing has persuaded the evil to leave. One day, we may have to shoot you.'"

Energlyn
Andy Bell, I must squeeze you into a tissue.

Erbistock
Another pub man.

"The digression is an exiled art form," he explained as I sucked on scotch. "Nowadays, we seek ordered clarity in sentences, not the unlassoed drift of the mind. There's no point deluding ourselves that our lives have structures or purposes. Neatness and pith have no place in fiction. I am a pervert. Mostly, my perversions remain stored within my cerebellum and have no place in the outer world. Except one. I like to touch ladies' knees on buses and trains. I make every attempt to disguise my delicate touchings as a series of sleepy hand misplacement errors, because I experience great shame and embarrassment at my actions. Perhaps some background would be welcome. No. The background is not necessary, since I have lost the impetus to speak background information. If truth be told I am excessively disturbed. I am a chocolate cake. And you are the bath into which I pour myself."

Erddig
Húsavík was mine. On the wind-whipped streets of that one-time coastal paradise I was raised. I biked around on a bike singing Elastica. I ran up hills with shoes and ran down them in socks. I fought terror by punching bucktoothed yokel children from Fossholl. I taunted the churching kids by tanking cans of Appelsín in front of their faces. I watched *Deep Throat* for the first time in Viktor Einarsson's shed. I ate pineapple chunks while lazing around in geothermal springs. As an adult, I took long aimless walks in a hoodie and petrified small children by standing in a shaft of sunlight that caught the ichor sheen of Yuki Chikudate.

Fairbourne
A madman accosted me on the A493.

"Did you know that the Canaanite king Adoni-Bezek had his big toes and thumbs cut off by King Arthur?" he asked.

"Nope."

"Did you know that standing on your tiptoes to reach high shelves causes more deaths per year than cancer?"

"Nope."

"Did you know that Tanya Donnelly from alternative pop-rock band Belly has five toes on her left foot and only five on her right foot? Did you know it takes three years for a leopard gecko's toes to grow back but only four hours for a shark's toes to grow back? Did you know that human beings are the only mammal with six toes on each shoe, and four toenails on each house? Did you know that a heelbone can deflect a bullet, but two heelbones can deflect a nuclear missile? Did you know the average hallux (big toe) on adult females weighs the same as a Volkswagen Sharan? Did you know the bits of lint and fluff that get stuck between your toes are a delicacy in Cardiff? Did you know the heel is a myth?"

"Yes."

"Did you know the bones in the toes are called the phalanges, named after Geoff Phalanges, who invented feet? Did you know the greatest cause of toe anguish is wearing the wrong shoes on your head? Did you know that syndactyly—two toes stuck together—is something to do with toes? Did you know that toe polish on toes is best worn on toes?"

"I wish you ill," I said, and pushed him into a mire.

Fairfield

I am a Cambrian coddiwompler.

Fairwater

I almost helped a geriatric cross the road then I remembered I have a face that would send Bashar Al-Assad running for his momma. I paid no mind as she slipped on black ice and lost her zimmer to a passing truck.

Felin Fach

'My Ex-Girlfriend's Literary Efforts' from Barrie Bartmel's *Poems of a Poltroon* (p.23):

> As the piece of sellotape
> holding up my rose-tinted spectacles
> wiggles loose
> I manoeuvre towards your oeuvre
> like a leonine critic
> circling an antelope
> and have to conclude
> that your imagination
> remains trapped within
> the confines of your parochial upbringing
> as your childish comic poetry
> yields indulgent smirks
> and your perfunctorily penned prose
> serves up skippable sentence
> after skippable sentence
> and I wonder to myself
> why love
> mangles our critical faculties
> making the lamest haiku
> a marvellous masterpiece
> or the fart-laden first draft
> a magnum opus
> as I turn to my current girlfriend
> to ask her what she thinks
> of this poem

Felindre

Paula Crouther, the Orcadian, said to me:

"Two cousins of mine wished to wed in the Kirkwall parish chapel. There are no rules against this in the Bible, even in the loopiest clauses of Leviticus, and the parish priest was hip to the groove when it came to homo-hetero-transsexual ceremonies and nuptials. However, the Orcadian Institute for the Preservation of the Sanctity of Marriage (shortened from a much longer name) protested that since two cousins wedding in 2010 was a reversion to barbarous practices, and as the church had turned a blind eye to gay marriage, to maintain some semblance of decency there should be no cousinly unions permitted. (Under their rules, cousinly unions *were* permitted thanks the historical precedent—their protest was made largely out of spite and to ruffle the overly cool parish priest's saintly feathers)."

"Take a breath, Paula."

"Thanks. Now, those cousins—Gerald and Geena—negotiated with the church and the OSPSM, reaching an agreement that the cousins might wed if one of them was situated on the UK mainland, i.e. Thurso, for the ceremony, and the marriage happened via Skype. This was arranged. Annoyingly, an administrative snarl-up and pressure from OSPSM agents meant the wedding was not permitted for another two weeks. Finding himself in Thurso, Gerald chose to stay and soak up the culture (Brecht and Beckett performed nightly at the local theatre), and met a charming lady named Mandy, an actress who played Winnie in *Happy Days*. Gerald, plush with new love, elected to remain in Thurso with Mandy, and abandoned the marriage. Geena's heartbreak reached the OSPSM, who started delaying the dates of possible marriages so that gays would meet other gays off the Orcadian mainland, and not pollute Orkney with their sodomite foulness, and in that way they won their pathetic little battle."

Felinfoel

Poor writers. Even a sentence slamming one's ineptitude at writing sentences has to be a fucking terrific sentence.

Ferndale

A local election is erupting in Wales's sallow face. Plaid Cymru, the social-democrats and usual electoral barnstormers, had become unpopular when Liechtenstein shellacked Northeast Wales with shrapnel, and responded with liberal calm, stating that merciless retaliation to avenge the slain was not the answer. The public needed a stronger, bloodier voice. The War Against Liechtenstein candidate, whose sole intention was to siphon Welsh tax into fighter planes and training an elite combat battalion, and to wage a vengeful war until Liechtenstein apologised or surrendered (the outcome was unclear), were strong contenders. The Conservative candidate was running on the usual ticket of plum-voiced patrician sensibleness riddled with unsubtle rhetoric regarding kicking foreigners in the nuts, using the recent catastrophe to win voters around to their policies of closing nineteen factories and selling off parts of Snowdonia to Rupert Murdoch "to create new media platforms". The Labour Party had sent in a manifesto that no one read. The Liberal Democrats could not afford to print their manifesto and had to rely on word of mouth. This pathetic shower of political cockupmanship almost made me come around to the idea of Icelandic occupation. (Then I remembered the Bergþórusons and their form of hipster ethnic cleansing. Chaos and raging bloodlust were better.)

Fernlea
I met Katrin the third time in her apartment. She fed me herring.

Ferryside
In the 1970s, living in London or Manchester made the likelihood of seeing some of the most prominent punk and post-punk pioneers for a pittance more probable. In the 2010s, the likelihood of seeing the most prominent musical pioneers is low, unless you accept the £50 ticket charge, the £10 parking charge, and bring a set of binoculars from which to view the band from your cramped seat in Row Z. Live music is dead.

Ffair Rhos
March 31st is when Katrin and I celebrate the anniversary of our mutual acceptance that we came together as a couple because no one else could stand our pockmarked complexions, and that love between us

would forever be impossible because biological resentment would always trounce any feelings of closeness or tenderness.

Ffaldybrenin

From *An Alternative History of Wales*:

    1043 AD: King forbids explorers to fold Earth at the corners.

    1200 AD: Pineapple farming makes Gwynedd prosperous.

    1317 AD: People are found revolting. Lord of Senghenydd recommends soap.

Fforest

I am staring at a hole in my embroidered block-stripe sock and wondering if Katrin's father's racism might have subconsciously infected her otherwise carefully calibrated system of universal misanthropy.

Ffoshelyg

I am unsure in what precise manner I loathe myself. I should loathe myself, what with the levels of ugliness viewed as a public health hazard, and the social pain these levels of ugliness cause. But I loathe more the shallow-minded response to this ugliness, and the public's assumption that I should remain unseen for their sake, more than I loathe the fact of the pustules and their pusiness. I loathe too the fact that I loathe these people, as people like the people I loathe *expect* me to loathe the people who loathe me—a fact I resent. This leads me to conclude that the thing I loathe is loathing itself, and since I am unable to unloathe loathing itself, I am trapped with a conceptual and weird form of loathing, which makes me loathe myself even harder. As a rule, loathing myself and everyone else covers all bases.

Ffynnongroyw

Here, feral children hunt for hands reaching from the rubble, take them in their own as if to show compassion, them chop them off with meat cleavers.

Fishguard

Having a riot in this here Saab, picturing the Bergþórusons, oiled up in their mankinis, bent over in the stocks, awaiting the surprise sodomy of a loved-up hippopotamus.

Five Roads

"Has anything interesting ever happened here?" I asked a pub random.

"Yes. In the noughties, singer Chris Martin visited the village with a famous woman when his limo took the wrong left at Heol Hen. This incident was spoken of for months and caused a huge spike in tourism," he said.

"Is that all?"

"Pardon me. I have not finished. Now, David and Darren Grasshead had long left the village to forge a path in the heady literary sphere of Inverness, struggling to make an impact with their thrillers set in local council departments and travel agencies, and sensed a chance to make an average living by exploiting Chris Martin's brief spotlight thrown on their homevillage. David returned first after catching the 11.29 train (Darren missed this due to an unexpected item in bagging area and no staff members on hand to resolve the problem—he had to take the 14.29 instead), and claimed his portion of their shared flat, setting up his desk and computer at the window overlooking the small wooded area situated beside the two larger wooded areas known as The Wooded Areas."

"Extraneous detail, old man."

"Yes, apologies. When Darren arrived, David was nine pages into his cash-in book *Five Roads: A User's Manual*, a short and humorous trip around the two interesting things to do in the village, primped with amusing and pornographic anecdotes from residents' personal histories. Darren set up his desk and began his rival title, *Five Roads: Less is More*, talking up the beautiful Carmarthenshire scenery, the rustic gastropubs, and most confusing roadsigns that might appeal to the average non-Cambrian visitor. Over the following week, with Chris Martin's visit still fresh in the public's minds, David and Darren completed and self-published their books, placing advertisements through mailboxes, making a respectable sum that covered their rent for the next two months."

"More narrative oomph, codger."

"Well. A non-fiction publisher picked up their respective books for nationwide distribution. David's outsold Darren's by six copies, leading to a festering resentment on Darren's part, having always been the slightly less talented, slightly less masculine, and slightly less vertical (not that to the outside observer, there was a marked difference between their respective talents—these were disparities built up over years of ranking minuscule traits, leading to this minuscule pro-David bias), and tension around the kitchen and bathroom. (Unlike their Inverness flat, this one had two bedrooms, so these grudges were not transferred into the realm of sleep and nightmares). These titles made them well-known in the village, and the closest thing Five Roads ever had to local celebrities. (An internet rumour that Siouxsie Sioux was born here was soon squashed with a pic of her birth certificate)."

"Ramble no more, wrinklèd one."

"Yes, so. David wrote a comedic novel, *Chester's Sou'wester*, about an accountant who loses his hat and undergoes an series of amusing mishaps in an attempt to retrieve the hat, such as selling his knuckles to a local consortium, while Darren wrote *In the Field of Danger*, a war thriller about a soldier struggling with his cowardice in the field of battle, who overcomes this cowardice to be macheted in the face in battle. Both novels were received with critical shrugs, and once again David outsold Darren by six copies (only seven copies were sold per author). An overview of the charity shop showed that Five Roads' residents preferred misery memoirs. David at once began an account of his poor and difficult upbringing as the hated sibling. Darren copied. There was an appetite for a romanticised view of the village as a bog-wallowing hellpit. Each brother sought to fulfil that vision in print."

"Please end this now, Grandpoppie."

"I . . . I can't remember what happened next."

"What?"

"I forget. The brothers either wrote their memoirs or never had the time. Or perhaps one of them went back to Inverness to have sex."

"So in short, this whole tale was a slow trickle of ear-swill? This tale was a ruse to shoot seventeen precious minutes of mine in the nostrils?"

"I like talking to people."

"Tell me the truth. Are you one of the Grasshead brothers?"

"Yes. But I can't remember which."

"I will lob a flecklet of pity at your pepper-and-salt as I depart," I said, lobbing my flecklet. It landed in his Guinness.

Flemingston

"Be content with a boxset," a shrewish Welsh said.

Flint

Nothing remains except rubble, twelve stark heaps of rubble, from which protrude sad reminders of this town's former existence, like the bent 'M' of the McDonald's logo, or a sliced cursive from the Tesco sign. The clean-up workers are eating their sandwiches on the banks of the River Dee. I walk past the fourth pile, and observe a cuddly panda soaked through with the blood of the dead. I feel a strange elation.

Four Mile Bridge

I knew this manic street thinker at work on the book *Living Under Bridges*. He postulated the posit that living under a bridge was a shortcut to complete mental equilibrium. He believed the bridge is a pathway not only between two places, but a pathway between life and death. The bridge situates one between living and not-living. He started writing as a hobo, sleeping under rumbling commutery motorway ones, eking out a hoboish semi-life with customary knapsack and pocket rum. He moved on to larger bridges, constructing a fort for himself, where he would listen to the thrum of passing life and think about how the heart is squeamish. As time passed, the temptation to hurl himself into the sea became more overwhelming. Living in limbo for that period of time forced him to make a choice between living or croaking. He hurled himself into the sea. I admired his intellectual rigour.

Foxhall

A stuttering lad stepped up to the podium to make a speech on the unfairness of laws. He overcame his lifelong stutter to bring a rousing message of peace and love to a clump of sneering locals. It was a simply transcendent moment. Then I remembered the songs of Maroon 5. My pleasure was pulped to a wet, shapeless mass.

Fron (Montgomery)

"A moral étude?" a man whispered at me in the pub.

"Go on."

"Four cads each lost an item. The first lost a cab, the second a can, the third a cap, and the last a cat. The cab-losing cad came upon a can. The can-losing cad a cat. The cap-losing cad a cab. The cat-losing cad a cap. The cab-losing cad was parched and consumed the can's contents. The can-losing cad wanted a cute companion and kept the cat. The cap-losing cad was miles from home and caught the cab. The cat-losing cad was in a hot climate and needed the cap. Several months later, the cads each lost a car. Since the cads worked in the same club as caddies, all four decided to co-rent a car and share the work drive. This became a pleasant routine until the car's cam broke and the car crashed into a tree, killing the cads. This tale might teach us the importance of compassion in a corrupt age."

Froncysyllte

Mother: "Your cascading fringe will not stop amoral bankers trousering the pensions of the pinched and sickly."

Garnant

Bergþórusons, one morning the plaintive wail of the rentier classes will penetrate the thick carapace of indifference protecting your brains, and make your heads explode like depth-charged watermelons.

Garndolbenmaen

I walked around this peaceful rural community, listening to the late-morning birdsong subside, watching uncomplicated rustic folk conduct their business, and I wondered if self-contained communities, if brought together in the spirit of egalitarianism, might show the world a more compassionate solution to bowelless capitalist living. If these simple folk might have the blueprint for a harmonious world, and if we follow their example, we might escape this bleak and troubled time in our history. Then I remembered Vince Vaughn. I drowned the thought in a sack and spat into the wind.

Gellioedd

On the train, I sat next to a chap with his muscular legs splayed in an arrogant V. I was squeezed into the window seat with mine folded and tilted at a right angle towards the window. I tried the method of nudging slowly, exerting pressure on the kneebone over a thirty-minute period, and was making progress correcting the violation when he reached for an ipod in his rucksack and forced the legs into a retreat. I hadn't the stamina to resist.

Georgetown

Read William Morris's *News from Nowhere* in the B&B vestibule. It is pleasant to remember that, in our outrageous and ill-mannered world, we have the potential to create utopian societies, where ephebes and red-cheeked Venii canter around village greens, exchanging flirtatious banter in Latin and Welsh, never once seeking to crush a pockmarked peasant under their well-shod hobnails for the mere titter factor. Morris's hallucinogenic utopian novel is like falling into a bed of soft blonde hair, or rolling around a meadow in one's shorts as the summer sun bronzes one's pert buttcheeks, and a kind-hearted auntie serves up a platter of cream tea with extra cream. As our planet approaches the certitude of fast-moving extinction via the rolling revue of autocratic thundercunts at the helm of most nations, an afternoon spent in this Victorian reverie is a soothing balm for the soul.

Gilfach
Bergþórusons, one morning the people of Iceland will hurl their mobiles and ipods and tablets towards your complacent smirking faces, and splatter your skulls across the heated floors of your human thoughtpods.

Gilwern
I used to work for an Icelandic tabloid, taking long-lens shots of bikinied Z-listers from bushes. I would sit in an office, zooming in closely on puppyfat, bruises, or any notable skin defects. I would shame the celeb for not possessing the silken skin of an angel every moment of every day. It is a form of betrayal. If more movies depicted what people actually look like our world might be less jabbery.

Glan-y-Don
Sometimes when I sneeze, a pimple erupts.

Glan-y-môr (Ceredigion)
This is what Emma Oust said to me:
   "I am the woman who most resembles rock musician and actress Courtney Love out of all women in the world. Despite not hailing from Portland, Oregan and having no American lineage, my likeness to the young Love is remarkable. I was working in an Oddbins in Poole when someone first pointed this out. Since I had failed in school (a poor head for facts) and ended up in low-paid servile work, my family and everyone else suggested I set up as a Love lookalike and capitalise on the coincidence. That's when the trouble began. Having never heard Love's music, or about her marriage to Kurt Cobain, I was shocked to learn about her career as a public nuisance, her exhibitionism, and tuneless vocals. I am a reserved person and have no particular fondness for attention. I therefore backed away from this career and started an HND in Flower Arranging."

Glan-y-nant
The people here are semi-inclusive reclusives.

Glan Conwy
The first pimple, Kevin Shields, popped up one week into teenhood. My father conveyed me to the backdoor with a solemn paternal gait and, under the strabismic red porch lights, said to me: "Magnus, I have some difficult truth to lock into your lugholes. You are a victim of genetic roulette. The males in our family belong to a long line of boil-inheritors. Your grandfather had a head voted Most Mutated in a 1928 poll. Son, from now on, you will have to struggle. Life will not be the same for you as other men. As you develop, your friends will start to shun you. You will walk into rooms and elicit murmurs and titters and sharp intakes of breath. You will spook small children at parks and beaches. People will strategically move away from you on public transport. You will be passed over for work and might never find satisfying emploi. You will not have success with women. The sexual world is not a realm in which you might freely participate, if you understand my meaning. Kevin Shields is the first star in a furious cast of vicious facial tormentors. You will have to learn to tolerate the cruel nicknames. Pimple Longspotting. The Magic Pus. Spot the Dog. Zitti Pusitti. The Face the Boot Stomped on Forever. Pimple Simon. Sacherwart. Blackheadbanger. Papule New Guinea. You must steel yourself for a tough, long, and lonely life." I thanked my father for his candour. My childhood had ended.

(No one called me a single one of those names. The real ones were far worse).

Glanamman
The people here want to murder the newborns of Liechtenstein.

Glascoed
On the fifteenth of each month, five talespinners spin their tales in The Tailspin pub. I sat there in a snood and listened to them.

The first was a frieze-clad oenophile in male form who spoke: "Claire was sat writing her thesis on molecular infometricals or something when she became extremely distracted by her breasts. My, what pleasant lacteal dugs I have, Claire thought. I could spend my life nourishing parched infants with these beauties and sending unsexed males into pitches of priapic madness with these well-proportioned milkbags. I will abandon this thesis on molecular infometricals or something at once and share my delights with the rest of the world. She moved to Newcastle, where she opened an office for those with infants needing succour and males needing a nippled orb to fondle for their amusement. She made over seven million pounds in the first week and opened a karaoke bar in Nigeria."

The audience received this in silence. It clunked like the carburettor on a vintage Dodge Charger having been crankshafted into oblivion. Two ladies in the front row snorted liquid fizz over the "nippled orbs".

The second was a shame-waisted aurorophile in female form who spoke: "Henning was an actress who longed to play the part of a teak cabinet on the stage. He decided, one day, to create the part for himself, since the role hadn't come his way. He wrote *The Teak Cabinet Monologues* in nine minutes. In his potting shed he built a teak cabinet from scratch with a backdoor so he could sit inside and fully, literally, inhabit the cabinet. On show night, five stagehands lifted him (as cabinet) onstage, before a microphone. For two hours, the audience sat rapt as the cabinet made no sounds except odd creaks or coughs from Henning inside. The play received lukewarm reviews and a cult following."

Two audiencers clapped. A plus-sized man wanted to whoop but the unenthusiastic clapping blocked the whoop at throat level.

The third was a wasp-hearted eurotophile in male form who spoke: "One time, eight-year-old Alice Leeward from Devonshire thought 'I am the Trade Union leader Bill Callahan!' She became the Trade Union leader Bill Callaghan. One day, the Trade Union leader Bill Callahan thought, 'I am a talking plastic chicken on a Nebraskan farm!' He became a talking plastic chicken on a Nebraskan farm. One day, a talking plastic chicken on a Nebraskan farm thought, 'I am a paperclip!' He became a paperclip and so lost the power of thought. We might extract from this the shiver of a moral."

A whoop escaped someone's lips. Four whoops followed. Soon most of the audience released unexpected whoops. This tale triggered a veritable Mexican wave of whoops and was perceived as the best so far.

The fourth was a skull-headed macrophile in female form who spoke: "In the following story, an architect drops his pencil at the feet of an attractive lady, Teri. We are about to begin. He's reluctant to reach down and pick up the pencil in case Teri thinks he's looking up her skirt. All right, let's start the story now. Michael is an architect. He is sitting at a table with several other architects at a convention of architects. As a speech is being made about architectural matters, he drops the pencil he was twirling in his hands to the floor. It lands at the feet of Teri, an attractive fellow architect wearing a slightly skimpy skirt. He is reluctant to reach down and pick up the pencil in case Teri thinks he is trying to look up her skirt and embarrassment ensues. In the story you have just heard, an architect named Michael was sitting twirling a pencil in his hands at an architects' conference. He dropped the pencil at the feet of Teri, an attractive female fellow architect in a short skirt. He was reluctant to retrieve the pencil in case Teri accused him of "peeping" up her skirt. Thank you for listening to my story."

The audience leapt from their seats and let rip a percussive strafe of appreciation with their mad clapping hands. Nine hundred whoops and one thousand bravos were heard across the hour of rapturous appreciation. Never in The Tailspin's history had such a tale of sparkling magnificence sparkled in their earholes.

The fifth was a sap-drenched plutophile in male form who spoke: "This is a realistic story. In this story, based on true-to-life events, Kevin sits in a pub and watches the football. Kevin enjoys the match until it becomes clear (having been spoken into existence only a sentence ago) he is a fictional character, so he decides to leave the story like in those clever metafictions by Flann O'Brien and Gilbert Sorrentino. Kevin says that, in real life, if he found out some bastard writer had written him into in a story without his knowledge, he'd be out of there so quick, the bastard would barely have time to wet his quill. This is a good point. It keeps the story true-to-life. But this leaves us with a dilemma. Since Kevin has left, there are no characters in this story. Any new character would soon become aware of his role as a fictional character and walk out. No narrative would take flight. This is essential for a story, you have to have willing characters. The solution is simple. I will put myself into the story, like in those clever metafictions, and watch the football. So there I am, in the pub, watching the football. But then it dawns on me that I hate both pubs and football, so I leave my story."

A cough followed. This cough signalled that the talespinner was an incompetent waste of room. The clear winner, the fourth one, had already hopped on her moped and was last seen eating ragù in Caerleon.

Glenboi
Overheard:
"Hi, Izzie. I met you once at the launch for some piddling book of poems in which I was published. Everyone flocked around you after the reading to hear your opinion on the poems and you said the collection was wonderful. I spoke to you about your contributing to a new story collection and you looked around the room like you couldn't wait to get away from me, contriving some hokey excuse about meeting your wife in the car park (at that time you were not married). I knew you were trying to avoid me so as to avoid having to stoop to working with such untested talent as us piddling poets. Why are you such a coward, Izzie-pops? You can smirk and praise a collection you haven't even read, but don't have the courage to refuse my offer? Perhaps you won't feel so self-satisfied when your latest book tanks, when I tell my friends and everyone I know (I have 2,383 Twitter followers) to boy-

cott your novels forever, perhaps you won't be so keen to make up a pathetic lie to escape working with me. Have a nice life."

Glyncorrwg

Coarse fishing and entitlement.

Glyndyfrdwy

Whenever Katrin is silent in a clump of damp thatch, I know she is recalling when her 67-year-old father called her a "fat-ankled facsimile broad."

Glynneath

This is what Oliver Hamm said to me:

"I looked down at the old penis last week and noticed it had turned orange. Mum wondered—had I dipped the old penis in a soft drink like Tango or Irn-Bru? Nope. Then how come the orange colour? Had I immersed it in orange paint, or had it been painted orange in some stag-night prank? Nope. Then how come the orange colour? Had I sleepwalked naked into a room containing a strong orange solvent of some sort? Nope. Then how come the orange colour? Had I been to a tanning salon where the UV lights were particularly strong over the old crotch? Nope. Then how come the orange colour? Perhaps this orangeness was a mere a trick of the light? Nope. It was orange, and that was that."

Glyntaff

Yes, I kicked a terrier in the face.

Goodwick

A gulp of cormorants swooped across the blood orange sky in a perfectly synchronised V towards the purring waters on a serene, peaceful August evening. I realised someone, somewhere, would see those birds and think: "I'd love to blow those flapping fuckers from the skies." The moment was ruined.

Gorslas

This is what Llana Plaine said to me:

"On Monday we had sex. It was more or less the same as the last time we had sex. We had no sex for two weeks, then we had sex on Wednesday. It was the same as the last time, if a little worse as Maximillian achieved a mere semi. We had no sex for the month following and then we had sex on Tuesday. It was better than the last two times, however, it had been so long since we had had sex, we failed to notice this marked improvement. We had no sex for another month, then we had sex on Thursday, out of mutual frustration and marital obligation. We had no sex for two months, then we split up for reasons of extreme sexual dissatisfaction. Sex, my bizarre friend, was no longer on our mutual agendae."

Greenfield

This is what Caroline Trikkle said to me:

"I scaled the top of Ben Nevis. Up there, I discovered the skeleton of Ron Wilson, my sister's cousin's father, who had perished in a unpredicted blizzard. Seeing this dead man put me off my victory, so I planted my flag and began the precarious descent. He had always been a fan of colourful shoes. In his collection, he had up to ninety-nine pairs, including a set of Italian loafers once worn by Fellini. If you called him a "shoe fetishist" he would reach over and punch you. I couldn't believe my luck. I won the lottery a second time, only nine weeks after the initial win. People said it was avaricious of me to keep playing the lottery, but if you have eight million, you may as well buy a thousand tickets and increase your odds, right? I bought a small island off the coast of Mexico, where I trained sheep to perform daredevil stunts, such as setting their fur on fire and forcing them to make a Houdini-like escape from their skin before they turned into itty bitty haggises. My mother tried to stop me from running away to become a world-renowned trapeze artist. Her enormous pimpled face, with its horrible hairs poking out, stood over my bed one night and said: 'If you leave, you're no longer my daughter.' I wasn't scared of this theatrical shit. I said: 'Biologically your argument is screwy.' She slammed the door and the next morning I left to pursue my career."

Groeslon

There is a plaque here on the tree where Liam Neeson once pursued a black swan.

Gronant

Sand dunes and the middle-aged.

Guilsfield

This is what Vaughan Grenade said to me:

"After six annums of career stagnation and consistent non-publication, I wondered if I could ever cultivate and maintain an erection again. I conducted an experiment with non-writer female Gretchen Mattis: a wispy creature with average diction and sluggish movement (I suspect masking a rheumatoid disorder). We rendezvoused in an eatery, the location unimportant, and ordered potato and leek soup with croutons. We talked about the canvii of Don Van Vliet and the ecstasy of early Kinks, then repaired to the Square for a romantic walk. After taking a kiss, I waved farewell and measured my ardour. My benchmark was Wendy Echt, the last female I had loved. She died in traction in 1999. From Gretchen Mattis, I experienced no cardiorespiratory quickening when our lips connected and no surge of blood to my penis indicating excitement. To confirm, I arranged a second date two days hence and, post-chips and sea bass, a trip on The Wheel, and two squirts of rum at the Rum Squiter, I invited her back to mine for sex. After seven minutes of kissing, Gretchen rubbed my crotchal area with her right hand for nine minutes, to no effect. I pictured Wendy Echt for six of those minutes. Still nothing. 'You can stop, Gretch. I have to fess. I was testing to see whether my time as a writer had rendered me a sexless, passionless, impotent eunuch. After this short experiment, it turns out that each refused story, each rejected manuscript, each career setback—on a daily, weekly, monthly, yearly basis—has withered my ardour to such an extent the ministrations of a cute woman like yourself are futile in the yielding of a simple erection.' Gretchen left halfway into the third sentence."

Gumfreston

I awoke from another violent tussle with Helga to a scornful Katrin, leaning on an elbow, amused at the blabbering noises I had been making.

"Another botched romp?" she asked.

"Yes," I said. "Helga." She regarded the urgent erection I sported.

"Shall we mask up for old time's sake?"

"K."

"I want Tiger tonight."

She retrieved two masks from the bedside cabinet. It had been our ritual, whenever we awoke ill-dreamed and lust-blazed, to have sex wearing the masks of people with whom we wanted to have sex, i.e. not each other. I had a mask made from a photo of Helga pinched from her Facebook page. Katrin had multiple images of the superhunks she paid on webcams to strip and touch themselves. This time, she selected the Aryan love-machine Tiger, star of the channel All White All Nite.

"I hate you," she said, six minutes into her pelvic assault.

"No, you hate yourself."

"Also true." She came using the shrill banshee noise she knew reduced the length and intensity of my own coming, then flopped off my flab in a hum of shame, sweat, and sneering.

"Why don't you kill yourself?" she asked.

"Because while I am alive," I said, reaching for water, "while I am reviled for having a face that inspires hate, I deserve the miniscule satisfaction I derive at terrifying children with my appearance. I solicit nothing except revulsion and pity from adults until I torment their sprogs. Then they see me, they see I exist, and the fear they feel for their children's safety is the fear I feel everyday at being judged and ostracised for simply being alive."

"So, in summary, your principal reason for living is to petrify small children with your horrible face?"

"And you? Forcing male beefcakes to crouch until their shanks ache? Hate-tweeting celebrities with photoshopped evidence of false hypocrisy? Pretending to be Claire Foy on Match.com?"

"I'm bored with your words." We were rehashing old snark. She rolled over and claimed 70% of the duvet.

Gurnos

Depressing to the point of extreme hilariousness. Most of the residents here choke on the titters in their mouths.

Gwaenysgor

On an icy December night, Helga Horsedóttir leans over to me, places her cold lips on my cheek, and I die.

Gwaun-Cae-Gurwen

Translated, means "whatever that means".

Gwernaffield

This is what DCI Whippoorwill said to me:

"I crouched to examine the corpse of a female toddler arranged with care along the harbour. Her outline had been pre-chalked by the killer, with a ring of daisies sewn into her dress, and a large boulder rammed into her insides, with a note attached: 'My name is Georgie. I like ponies and candyfloss. Nothing lasts forever. Merrily, we are all skittering towards the void.' I am a seasoned detective. I paused for a moment to weigh up the wherefores of this kill. Then I heard a ping on my mobile. I read the new email:

> Dear Mr. Whippoorwill
>
> Thank you for sending us your manuscript *Goddamn the Night*. Although we think your manuscript has potential, it is not something we can envision selling at the present moment.
>
> Best regards, Anne Hatchets

"I repocketed the phone. 'Scoop out the insides and bag them up,' I ordered the forensic team. 'I need a nap.' I stormed from the scene, using the two large powerful legs I possess to propel me towards the Daewoo, inside which I wrote this response to Anne Hatchets:

> You chomping mooks have no idea what you're talking about. This is the most exciting crime debut for years. This is the first cop thriller set *in the morning*. Every other cop thriller is set in the murky midnight hours in the rain. In this one, most of the murderous action takes place around 9.30am in the bright sunshine. You are utter morons to pass this one up.

"Next morning in the office, I scanned reports of the murdered toddler. The killer had mailed a rambling philosophical tract explaining his reasons for the murder, using Hegel and Kant as rationale for the snuff and listed several prominent cabinet members who had influenced him. I read a few sentences and tossed the rest on a stack of case files. I had a blistering headache. Anne Hatchets and her ilk have no clue what constitutes a ripping criminal tale. My novel has an innovative twist of brilliance. It is set in the *morning*, for heaven's sake. I will continue to shop this novel around the publishers with vehemence. I am an astonishing new voice on the scene. Tell everyone."

"All right," I lied.

Gwernesney

I am strolling in the woods with Helga. As we amble into an isolated copse, she raises her frilled white dress to reveal a smooth knicker-less bottom above her thigh-length stockings. She bends over a tree, and beckons me with a single index finger forward, inviting me to unleash the hard piston in my trousers, eager to penetrate her sweet, wet vagina. I commence this arboreal lovemaking with a passionate flourish, loading my lumber inside her with a hot and manly thrust. I work a steady rhythm as she moans and pants, her nails scraping against the bark. As I am nearing climax, I notice that Helga has vanished, and that my wood is in the wood, that I am penetrating the tree, and upsetting an army of termites, who mount an assault on my member. I am unable to extricate myself from the tree, no matter how much I push and push. I can only watch in horror as the termites devour my cock. In the distance, Helga looks on, laughing. She has the head of a termite. I awake in despair.

Gwynfe
I chose to eat like a cat. I walked into restaurants, parted the skirts of salmon, left my chair, strolled around the restaurant sniffing other people's food, returned to my chair for another nibble, prowled around outside, then tried to return inside to complete my meal. I was blocked by a sweating server.

Gwytherin
Translated, means "a wild horse on a collision course".

Halkyn
Translated, means "Walter Kronkite in a splendid arraignment".

Hanmer
Barrie Bartmel is now receiving a posthumous eisteddfod in the media. It is far easier to laud a cadaver with one published volume to his name than to support a struggling poet through volume after volume. Let the critical vultures feast.

Harford
People tell me this place escaped the Nazis using lasers.

Harlech
My father mistook ice-fishing in silence and random winks as we ate our evening plokkfiskur for a solid foundation of unconditional love and support. It happens.

Hasguard
Helga, the force of the love I have for you could frazzle the rings off Neptune.

Hawarden
I am not a victim. I am a contemptuous, exasperated outcast trapped in an unsavoury cycle of self-hate, reckless rudeness, and sexual perversion, performed with consummate inconsistency in the hope of exacting some incoherent revenge on three indifferent assholes four hundred miles away. Yes, all right. I am a victim.

Hay-on-Wye
I watched a man staggering from the off-license, vodka in hand, pumped to the hilt with ethanol, waving a sheaf of papers towards a pram-pushing mother, who recoiled from the sight as the man, feeling something arising in his throat, hunched over the pram and vomited copiously onto the baby's face, as the mother screamed. A stream of seemingly endless spew, a greenish-red mix of vodka, cheeseburger, salad niçoise, and red cabbage, completely soaked the screaming baby, flowing for far longer than you would have thought humanly possible, to the point the pram was soaked through, and the baby floated over the side. The mother pushed the man away, who tripped and tumbled into the kerb. Rising in a funk, he shouted "Sorry!—*hic!*—Sorry!", and tripped on his manuscript, causing a second wave of sick to stream over the woman's face, and another wave to coat the infant swaddled in her arms. It was to some horror that he noticed his trousers and pants had come loose, and that he had an erection. It was Richard Allcroft. Nicolas Lezard in *The Guardian* called his first novel "a breathtaking evocation of postwar Europe in the tumult of major constitutional change."

Hayscastle
I swear I saw the staggered apparition of John C. Reilly coming over the hill.

Hendredenny
Katrin: "I encouraged my father's adultery. I told him, 'Your male organs are pre-programmed to seek fresh female secretions. The brief

transfer twice a week from your wife's organs to mine indicates a healthy, zestful genital progress, and that is medically probable.' "

Heneglwys
The Quantum Scale of Facial Catastrophes (in five phases):

Quantum 2—"The Quasi-Quasimodo": Your secretion levels have been rammed into overdrive. Unexpected blackheads and warts have invaded your skin like a race of crazed Mongol Mujahedeens. These unpoppable pop-ups cannot be concealed with foundation and might take the form of a pulsating papule on your neckline, a prominent pustule on your eyelid, or a bubbling blackhead on your nose. Wherever placed, passing strangers will lock onto that embarrassing bump at once, and back away, as if your unfortunate burden was contagious. You will need to drink Stolichnaya.

Hengoed
If the past 200,000 years of female subjugation could make a noise, that noise would be Babes in Toyland's 1992 LP *Fontanelle*.

Hensol Castle
O, Helga, I am kissing your knees. I am running my tongue all up your summer-bronzed legs. I am working my way up your chemise, and lapping at your beautiful cunt. I am lapping at your cunt until I realise your cunt has turned into a suppurating boil. My mouth is filled with pus and you are standing in a perspex box, staring at me with the expression of someone who has trampled a dog to death on purpose.

Herbrandston
Barrie Bartmel had the sense to kill himself to ensure that no new poems would skew the boneheaded interpretations of the ones he published.

Hightown
I am embarrassed.

Hirwaen
I tend to vote for sociopathic ideologues. Fast-tracks human extinction.

Hoaldalbert
I skulk around inside a headache, rubbing raw the unsalvable scabs of the past. A father, a mother. An ice-cold crevasse. A polar outpouring. A sea of wincing faces, a wave of crashing and crippling rage and shame. The simpering patience of pseudo-hearted strangers. The locking of doors. The whispering in rooms. The frozen smile of an ageing stranger and her frothing atrocities of the heart. The longness of the world. The shortness of the world. Futile scratchings up the hundred-foot well of loneliness. The reassuring clamour of soon-to-be-dead things. The matterlessness of stuff. The mattersnotness of them. A hellish sun. A soothing sheet of rain. A series of rut-pocked roads leading from unhome to unhome. The illusion of home, the laughable, slappable illusion of home.

Hodgeston
Be afraid, Burundi! Icelandic corporate fascism in the warm slippers of liberal democracy is coming!

Holywell
Here, rag and bone men thrash their wooden sticks at feral pigeons while sifting through the rubble for a tub of lard.

Holt
A young soprano performed an a cappella rendition of Leonard Cohen's 'Dance Me to the End of Love' at an open mic night that stunned all those present. We sat in amazement at her broken lovelorn voice, as though she had stared unblinking into the blackest recesses of the heart, and emerged with this precious, haunting gift. I realised someone, somewhere, would hear this and think: "That's so fucking boring. Put on some Lou Bega!" The moment was ruined.

Holyhead

It is no exaggeration to say that Wales has been pimp-slapped by recent history. Following the controversial decision to commandeer parts of the countryside for the temporary "storage" of new chemical elements, the so-called "malcogens" (a series of unstable liquids devised in a Moscow bunker), a squall erupted over Snowdonia. One Wednesday, known as The Night of the Black Puff, the malcogens collided to create a series of animal, vegetable, and mineral mutations on unsuspecting things that were alive. The first mutation occurred near Penmachno, where one hundred people lost their elbows as the malcontent malcogens (in invisible gas form) wafted towards the Penmachnoians. These elbows roamed the hills of Snowdonia, feasting on eagles and rooks, and harming civvies by springing from nests into their groins. As I arrived at Holyhead, the first words whispered to me were "beware the elbows". I stepped from the vessel in a clench of paranoia, worried the Welsh might assault me with their elbows in some violent elbowing ritual reserved for foreigners.

As it happened, the famous coastal town had been inundated with a non-specific evangelical religionist cult called God(∞) who liked to wear halos and toeless sandals and worshipped no actual He in particular. The concept of a God serving up infinite love was enough for them. The theological specifics were irrelevant. I leapt into the first pub I saw and slurped lukewarm minestrone, becoming increasingly mindful of halo-headed people in beige smocks screwing up their faces and whispering anti-me things in huddles. I was mopping up the last of the soup with a half-slice of wholemeal when a tall unbearded man called Hogarth asked if I might follow him into a room that he had in the pub's fragrant rear.

"You new here?" he asked.

"Yep," I said. "What is it? I've been travelling without alcohol and I would like to tank up on tequila tout suite," I said.

"Listen, friend. I'm the leader here, and we . . . we've been talking. Your extreme facial . . . hiccups are testing our non-specific faith. We are conflicted. We are used to spreading our inspirational message among attractive people. Look at our apostles. These aren't twelve-shepherds'-pies-and-a-flagon-of-beer bods. These are well-toned well-flexed kale-and-spinach-smoothie bods. I suppose we seek a base level of sexiness in our religion. It is shameful to admit," Hogarth said. He stroked his beardless face and made the usual unapologetic frown common to all who want not to see mine (face).

"Hmm. Hogarth. This religion seems to me to lack the semblance of a fucking conclusion. You can't have Ganesh and Allah and Yahweh in one big cuddly love-stew. You sound like a clod of convictionless hippies," I said.

"Cool accent. Are you from Sweden?"

"And what is the purpose of placing the lemniscate in parentheses? In fact, what is the purpose of the lemniscate, period? God is ∞, no? It seems, with this boneheaded approach to serious theological matters, your cult is an excuse for beddable simpletons to screw each other and take a lordly attitude to others. And the halos and smocks are hardly representative of the entire panoply of world Goditude."

"Hmm," Hogarth said, having not understood word one of me. "This is a worrying scone. We are burning with love's heat. We like a particular sort of loving hotness. We will have to ask you kindly to leave."

"Go asshump Allah, Hogarth. To hell with your halo-wearing beige-botherers. I've been in Wales for twelve minutes, you smirking twig. I want a vodka and scotch. I will be ordering several and then I will be leaving."

Honddu Isaf

This is what Carlton Grace said to me:

"I returned home, and after four unsuccessful attempts at recalling my password, I entered the multimillion dollar social media site. The first status was from a teenage cousin who wrote 'WOOT FOUR B's and a C in my exams!', adding a line of emojis including a party hat, a diploma, a pair of shades, and an ice cream. I wrote: 'Stop showing off. Other people who haven't done this well will find your post irritating or upsetting. And I don't see how an ice cream has any relevance to decent exam results.' This comment was fourth in line, and nineteen others followed with one or two-word messages of support. The remark stood out as the one with no exclamation points or upbeat sentiments, and my cousin did not reply, or 'like' the remark. The next status was a link to an article on a politician who was cutting benefits with the word 'Outrageous.' I wrote: 'You are always posting links to finger-pointing articles that have no effect but to make the reader feel hopeless or peeved. There is no point sharing this sort of thing. I am fed up looking at other people's political opinions or despairing rhetoric. Please keep it to yourself.' This again went unremarked upon. The next status was a picture of an old colleague next to a friend. I wrote: 'I'm not interested in seeing this person's face. I have no idea who this person is and I don't want to see them smirking at some remark made that I was not present to appreciate.' I continued to do this on each status. Some of the comments were vicious. To one woman who kept posting selfies: 'I am sick of this parade of vanity. These endless staged photos of you drooling over yourself, eager to show how awesome, attractive, and cool you are on near daily basis.' This received a stinging fuck-you response, which I was pleased to receive, as this was the one interaction I had had with this person in two years, and it was nice to reconnect before she blocked me. The next morning I logged on I noticed thirty-nine people had unfriended me, nine of them relatives. I sank into a depression. I repeated the process the next day. I had no friends left by the end of the week."

Horeb

I met a woman calling herself the Bardess of Horeb. She told me a tale:

"There was a typist (the typist of this tale) from Horeb known for her prudishness who made deliberate typos when typing out words with illicit syllables, such as 'titular', which contains the word 'tit', a slang term for female breasts. She was employed to type a tale titled 'The Titular Typist' and changed this to the 'The Ticklish Typist' to avoid the titular torment. This typist was soon sacked and replaced with a typist whose sensitive skin made her at times too ticklish to type, a condition aggravated by typing out T-words. She was employed to type a tale titled 'The Ticklish Typist' but in her paranoia at drawing attention to her condition, changed this to 'The Titular Typist'. She was soon dismissed. The titular typist was hired to correct the mistake of the ticklish typist, who at once fixed the error and restored 'Ticklish', and likewise the ticklish typist fixed the titular typist's error, restoring 'Titular'. Sadly, in their haste, both typists misspelled 'typist', writing 'tpyist' and 'typsit' in their haste to correct. Both typists were sacked and thereafter were unable to find paid work as professional typists."

Houghton
Helga Horsedóttir, for you, I would take the outstretched palm of a leper leaving the land for sorrowful quarantine.

Howey
I am sorry to report that the pachyderm was lost.

Idole
People tell me Don DeLillo spat on a coaster here.

Jameston
Stereolab never recovered from the loss of Mary Hansen.

Johnstown
Slouched in Offa's Dyke, sipping a banana milkshake in the lying sunshine, I pictured a footslogger in the Mercian army, on orders from Anglo-Saxon king Offa, peeping over to spot lurking Powys invaders, and lobbed him a sympathetic " es h l!" as I rammed a longsword up his nostril and parted his head from his neck. There are millions of people like me, waiting for the next war to partake in wanton bloodshed and have dramatic sanguine deaths, fighting for a future we will fortunately not have to experience.

Kenfig
Slogan: "Where the automotive industry comes to die."

Kidwelly
I am the whirling dreidel of pestilence.

Knighton
I read how a single mother of four who volunteered on the weekend with the fire service saved two pensioners from their fiery ends, and refused the £20,000 thanks they offered afterwards. It was a truly selfless moment of human compassion. Then I remembered the songs of Papa Roach. My pleasure was pulped to a wet, shapeless mass.

Laleston
Translated, means "open a vein in the sun and contemplate".

Lampeter
Helga, I dreamt that you touched me and I soiled myself.

Lampeter Velfrey
Helga Horsedóttir, for you, I would assist an arthritic box-stacker with a pack of six-litre sparkling water.

Laugharne
Beth Orton is the sound of the Icelandic middle classes.

Lawrenny
There is a plaque here outside the cottage where Alan Coren once borrowed a lug wrench.

Leeswood
The last Catatonia album is a wambling snotball of an LP. Punch me.

Letterston
A poet who refused to blurb Barrie Bartmel's bestselling collection is now on TV blowing smoke up a cadaver's fundament. There is no redemption for the real artist.

Liddeston
Hey, Bergþórusons! The housebound ex-miners whose throats are riddled with pneumoconiosis cannot *wait* to hear the postrock of Sigur Rós pumping through their stereos when the "rebranding" takes place.

Litchard
As I went door-to-door to show people the latest Quantum IV pimple (Pimpo da Neblina), I met a woman called Sally Forth who suffered from agoraphobia and anaemia. She was exceedingly pleasant to me, identifying a fellow sufferer of life-plague, and I was exceedingly, screamingly terrified of her, as she was a full feminine female, and I could not work with womankind. My pose of affected indifference in the face of their lovely faces was merely a means to conceal my shuddering horror of coming within a nine-mile radius of their saucy bottoms. I lived in terror of any movement that might be misconstrued as sexual. My sort (the repulsive, the horror-show) have a tendency to become lecherous perverts, so sexually parboiled that any pinch of bosom might turn us into violent clawing rapists, and although I seethed with lust for every attractively showcased neck, every sensuously helical ear, every milky-skinned shin, I could never show myself to be remotely interested in any woman anywhere. We are expected to live as happy eunuchs, our facial volcanoes somehow nulling the fact of our fully functioning libidos. We must never let on that our rampant hard-ons torment our sleeping and waking nightmares, that our enforced exile from sex turns us into crazed and frenzied masturbators. I have masturbated in more places than there are places. I have had illicit romps with a young Nancy Pelosi by the Westfjords. I have had a nine-way conga bang with the classic Fleetwood Mac line-up in the Burger King toilets. I have meatended more yummy mummies than there are yummy meats to eat with mummies. I have inserted my unblemished fantasy member into more holes than there are holes with women attached. If anyone for a second thought I might even contemplate anything as small as an innocent, friendly shoulder-tap to a fe-

male, their faces would snarl up and their skin would contort, as images of my boils weeping upon the milky breasts of helpless damsels came into their minds, my snorting Quasimodo body ramming into the virginal portals of a defenceless nymph. And the women themselves, having made their initial horror-faces, having inched into the begrudging realm of socially-semi-expected acceptance of my ugliness, tend to perform sexually hostile backing-away motions, shielding their breasts, and crossing their legs, as if my boils might suddenly seize control of my limbs in public places, and pull them towards the women for spontaneous rapes in Costa. As a consequence of this exile, I have the radial jitters whenever encroaching on any y-axis. I have no intention of completely alienating the other sex, thanks to the deep burrowing of Helga Horsedóttir into my affections, and the hope that I might somehow, someday, be facially adequate enough to stammer love into the ears of an unrepulsed and far less attractive woman, probably in her early 50s. Sally Forth belonged to the class of troubled woman far too involved in their own toxicities to care that I was hideous, the sort who secretly welcomed someone clearly drowning in a larger wave of universal rejection than herself, who could take some personal comfort at not being the most burdened wretch in the world, as they probably previously imagined themselves. I had a cup of tea in her cottage. As her every minutely kind word pooled into my ear, I wondered if I might stay here, in this flocculent nook, supping weak tea and loving her with more ardour than there was ardour to love. I finished my tea and hit the Saab, urinating against her fence first.

Little Milford

The people here want 2G broadband.

Llaingoch

From the parish Twitter: "I urge that Wanker Wilson take a few minutes to flatten the parish with a Panzer. His sermons are ripped off from Robert Burton and Thomas Merton so it isn't like the dude is locked in his room in eternal contemplation. Send in the mafia."

Llanarmon Dyffryn Ceiriog

I wrote a scathing review of the napkins in a Welsh restaurant. As I hit 'send', following two hours writing and rewriting, I realised how unamusing I was.

Llanarth

Katrin: "Are you thinking about putting your penis in Helga's ear?"

Llanasa

If this village were a condiment, it would be a Dutch Groningen mustard with a monounsaturated fat content of 0.6g.

Llanbadarn Fawr

I squealed for nine seconds in a transept.

Llanbadoc

A picture of Ross Perot was hidden here.

Llanbedr-Dyffryn-Clwyd

Translated, means: "I once knew this wench whose brain exploded out the back of her head. It happened at the bus stop on Hanover Street, Edinburgh. Her name was Trixie, which wasn't her real name. No, her real name was Trixilina Dixie III. So, oui. That brain went boom-splat. The incident came as a surprise to me, as I had been in Avalanche records a moment prior, haggling over the RRP of Right Said Fred. Even weirder was that Fred and Richard Fairbrass were bare-knuckle fighting outside in a cube. Odd. I trundled to the bus stop, thinking how human existence was a continual pull between deprivation, disappointment and disgust, vs. illumination, incandescence and love. I was, at the time, in lust with a woman named Biro. Her legs were pens—each toe a different colour—and I snuck her into lectures and libraries. Trouble was, one morning her ink ran dry, and she eloped with a sleazy octopus named   . This is when I first spotted Trixie. She was leaning over a bank vole from Portugal, helping the bank vole with its benefit claim form. I was hopping up and down, hoping to snog face with a one-legged girl on a pogo stick. It never transpired. What I did observe was a tattoo on Trixie's leg that read DÉCOR IS FUTILE. I learned from a friend that she was at war with interior designers. This war lasted months. Her house was painted when she was out, blueprints smuggled into her drawers, men fired paint at her in the street. One night, an agent planted a quarter of TNT in her cheek. The TNT had been deactivated, so no boom-boom ensued. For weeks, however, the interior designers had been stealing petunias from Nicola Barker's lawn, which was not politic in the slightest. Trixie responded with a controversial protest painting made from TNT sticks. The interior designers went "Pffft!". Trixie pushed the trigger, and that was that. But enough silliness. How are you, sweetie pie? Have you been burped today?"

Llanbedrog
Translated, means "neck-snapped in Volvo smash".

Llanbradach
Yes, Bergþórusons, I have used prostitutes. The first time was in Malmö, that half-timbered Swedish paradise, aged seventeen. I contacted a private escort named Magenta and acquainted her in English with the situation: to avoid humiliation I would wear a balaclava, like a sexual burglar, and on no account was she permitted to steal a look at my Quantum IVs. As a trespasser in the sexual world, hoping to avoid militaristic reprisals, I thought this an apt solution. Magenta charged extra and I lost my virginity inside my sweaty, prickly headwear, a voyeur in my own sexual life, which I would remain.

Llancadle
"I spit on Prince Hans Adam II," a spindly man said.

Llancayo
Mother: "You can right a million wrongs, son, this won't make you any less contemptible."

Llandanwg
I used to sit there, my rod rootling round the ice-hole, hoping my father said something to me across the course of an hour.

Llandarcy
I am in a B&B. I am sucking a knee. It is mine. I am on something. A ketamine calzone with crinoline sprinkles? A parabolic roti with Cornish ions? A mismanaged pie with boolean carrots? A squelching taco with rescinded decimals? A compliant aubergine with mumbling viands? A yammish yam with yammy yams and the yammiest yam in town? I am probably vomiting on a napkin as I write this.

Llandawke
There is a plaque here on the manhole that George C. Scott once plummeted down.

Llanddaniel
You know, Helga, I would even be nice to your kid. I would attempt to find her inane burblings interesting, I would pretend her artistic efforts were precocious, I would share in that belief of yours that your kid was somehow special, not merely a standard-issue Icelandic bourgeois daughter primed for middle-management. I would try, Helga.

Llanddeiniol
My mother, on my fourth birthday: "From this moment onward, I will no longer be providing the means with which you navigate the wilderness of your childhood through instructional toys or books. You must position yourself on a self-determined cultural and psychosexual axis, free from the casual childhood signifiers of sex that might end up your torturers in adulthood."

Llanddeiniolen
This is what Sal Bendex said to me:

"I love fuck-ups. Current fuck-ups, future fuck-ups, ongoing fuck-ups. The skill and range of these relentless bumblers is exhausting. I love how fuck-ups come to me with their panicked expressions, like paranoid squirrels protecting their secreted nuts, and make extravagant hand gestures while explaining to me in stuttering speech about their latest failed schemes and squished dreams. Their adorable hopefulness that I might rescue them a third time from their endless self-perpetuating modes of destructive behaviour, and the guilt in their darting eyes masking the shame and guilt at having failed to relaunch their mostly miserable lives, and those begrudging nods of thank you when I let them back into my house. I am Sal Bendex. I take control so they don't have to. Living is too tough for my fuck-ups. I am their keeper, protector, surrogate father. All I ask is that they return to me, always."

"I see."

"In 1999, I opened The Centre For Perpetual Failure, a private organisation to assist those who are disgusted by living and who might otherwise commit suicide or turn to substance abuse to cope with the hellishness of having to get up and breathe for another twenty-four hour period. The Centre preaches the fuck-up as a way of life, as a form of rebellion against the diabolical necessities of living. Those who are looking to reform their behaviour are not encouraged to sign up (in my experience people rarely change), because what we offer at the Centre is downtime between each fuck-up's latest attempt to succeed in life, and suggest ways they might improve themselves that they are likely to bungle. Those interested in really pulling their lives together are offered a leaving payout, and are banned from returning if they fuck up. You might argue that because these people have a safety net and one purpose in life—to fuck up—that they become successes through their skill at fucking up and always returning to the house in tears, etcetera. Not so. At the Centre, we train our fuck-ups to think succeeding is better and send them out with the intention to make it in the world. The advice we offer is tailored beyond their coping abilities, so when they return the remorse and pain is genuine. Those we suspect of milking the system for free and easy living are immediately turfed out and banned."

"Oh."

"I am Sal Bendex and this is how I live my life. I care little what people think of me."

Llanddewi Velfrey

The people here want to leave.

Llanddona

I see: the retreating form of Helga as a langspil is heard in queer corners.

Llanddulas

Paul Crouther, the Orcadian, said to me:

"Things were snailing along at *The Orkney Bugle* for hot-blooded hack Magthorf Harcus. The summer boom had passed, his scoops fading into paper lore: *Québécois Tourist Too Fat for Mine Howe*; *Pterodactyl Remains Unearthed at Skara Brae*; *Kirkwall Jamboree a Roaring Success*; *George Mackay Brown's Ghost Spotted Over Loch of Stenness*; *Old Man of Hoy Might be a Young Woman*; *Papa Westray Flights Delayed*. In the autumn and winter months, stories that weren't wind, rain, or snow-related were scarce. He struggled through September writing these: *Mouse Found on Eday*; *Girl Injures Ankle in The Shore*; *Fourth Tesco Superstore to Open in Kirkwall*; *Excessive Sand at Broch of Gurness, Complains Man*. In desperation, Magthorf manufactured stories by flexing the same imaginative muscle as island Bard George Mackay Brown. He began by travelling to the mainland, stealing a zebra from an enclosure in Aberdeen, slaying the creature, and returning to Orkney to deposit the carcass outside the house of noted racist Thornus Sabiston."

"Take a breath, Paul."

"Thanks. Taking snaps of the slain zebra laid outside Thornus's shed, Magthorf ran to his editor with the jpegs and a scandal was faked. Thornus denied ownership of the zebra, blaming the Vikings and coloureds for its presence. Magthorf printed that Thornus maimed a zebra as part of a hate campaign against non-Orcadians. In the article, Thornus was non-quoted: 'I hate the coloureds and whops. I butchered this zebra in protest to show how much I want them exterminated.' The liberal Orcadians were outraged. Magthorf continued to deposit more dead creatures in the shed, filling up the paper daily with updates of Thornus's beastliness. This soap opera kept the paper's circulation up until the stories of snow density returned, culminating perfectly in Thornus's suicide following months of ostracism and hatred. The technique had been so successful, Magthrof would use it again the following year to spite his ex-girlfriend. He tucked a savaged ostrich into her sheets one night."

Llandegveth

The writer Vaughan Grenade was blocked up bad. He said:

"I have a Greek wife, Eleni Alexandrou. She motivates me with insults. For example, this morning she taunted: 'Look at you, sitting there limp over your keyboard with that miserable frown on your face. Your problem, apart from your lack of motivation, originality, and humour, is that you are whelk-licking hobodaddy, a stationary smurf with no mirth.' I would then kiss her and write four chapters. And later, when the block returned, she said: 'I have read your previous novels, and honestly, my friend, you'd be better off writing advertising slogans for baked beans. Our children resemble ricket-ridden hobosprogs at the school gates, and you could change this.' I love my Greek wife, Eleni Alexandrou."

Llandegwning

I made a pronouncement that no one heard.

Llandeloy

'Angela' from Barrie Bartmel's *Poems of a Poltroon* (p.15):

> You are a 48° angle
> in a 99° world
>
> You are a snapped spoke
> on the bike of time

You are a broken biscuit
in a three-star hotel room

You are a spent vote
in a persnickety election

And I love you, Angela,
you silly bitch

Llandewi Skirrid
I made a long croaking sound in a narthex.

Llandinam
Listened to 'We're an American Band' by Yo La Tengo twelve times in bed. I sat up, stared at the floral wallpaper and the copper statue of St. David, then lay back and played it another forty-seven times. Sleep came.

Llandrillo
Overheard: "Mitchell, there's something you should know. I'm not your biological mother, I'm your kidnapper."

Llandrindod Wells
Yes, I sneered at a moorhen.

Llandruidion
I have this imagined conversation where I say, "Helga, I want to nibble your lovely black hair," and she says, "You are a weirdo and I will phone the police if you are not off my lawn in four seconds," and I say, "But Helga, you are in my imagined conversation, surely you should reply with some loving entreaty?" and she says, "No, even in your imagined conversation, I will not surrender to the touch of your monstrous hand," and I say, "This suggests that I have been so worn down that I cannot even bend my imagination to succumb to my pathetic fantasies," and she says, "That about sums it up, you disgusting freak."

Llandyfaelog

An obese, wind-beaten, fag-puffing couple are wheezing along the pavement in the pissing wet. The woman blithely steps into the path of a passing truck, and her husband makes a heroically successful effort to yank her chubby shanks back towards safety. "That breaks my fucking heart," Katrin says strangely.

Llandysul

Let the planet die, Iceland. You are wasting your time.

Llanelidan

I met the editor of a periodical who was under enormous pressure to launch a special issue on immigrant plight. He read stories from Iranian and Syrian and Afghani and Macedonian ex-pat writers and thought them utter twaddle. He knew the issue was being published to exploit the topical topic of war-blasted refugees, and the issue was sheer worthiness over innovation. The writing was, for the most part, heartrending true tales of lost relatives in various terrible wars (which was not in itself a fault, only the standard of writing was poor). He was irritated that a Welsh periodical was having to waste space on a hackpack of misery memoirs, soaked in the liberal tears of a left-wing masthead. He would have preferred to publish stories about lusty farmers. He was writing a sex comedy set in Bryncoch.

Llanelly

A revolting mansion and pottery.

Llanengan

DREAM [48]: I embark on a series of long-lens photos of Helga in repose at her bay window in summery outfits. In every image, she appears several stones fatter in a niqab and clodhoppers.

Llanerch-y-Mor

I only violate you in my dreams, Helga. The prospect of receiving your tenderness is too painful.

Llanfabon
Explosions and a train station.

Llanfachraeth
Translated, means "a hotel with invasive bedbugs".

Llanfaethlu
It seems that most people, vrooming along B-roads in the 2.49 mizzle, are struck numb at the fact their lives so far have been composed with outrageous slackness, and that no awareness of this will alter their flight paths to oblivion.

Llanfairpwllgwyngyllgogerychwyrndrobwyllllantysiliogogogoch
Translated, means: "So much more than a photo op beside the sign of an unpronounceable compound word!"

Llanfihangel-y-pennant
I entered the parish church and sat on a pew, wondering if an uncorrupted message of love and compassion, whether from a priest or an atheist, if it penetrated into the most embittered skull on the planet, might rescue our world from the belching mess of sin and self-interest, and people might break free from their patterns of greed and neediness, and unite to heal the world. Then I remembered Roseanne Barr. I drowned the thought in a sack and spat into the wind.

Llanfihangel Penbedw
People tell me this place is suboptimal.

Llanfugail
I see: a broken pencil under the settee, as I lollop on the floor staring up my mother's skirt.

Llanfwrog
I was urinating in a field when I heard a cricketesque rustle in the weeds. Having forgotten I had stepped into a nation at siege from

the rogue elbows of petrochemical catastrophe victims, I was unprepared for the scabbed killer that sprung from the weeds, whizzing over-shoulder onto the roof of my Saab, then retreating under the chassis for a second rev up. I had scant time to flee unzipcocked to the front door of the cottage on whose land I had been pissing. "Elbow! Elbow!" I called as I palm-thumped the door and poked my cock indoors. The elbow returned to the weeds as an unruffled Welshman offered his stuporous air, slategrey chequered cardigan, and 6.59-stubble at the open door.

"Oh. Elbows again, is it?" he said. He hoicked a shotgun from a coathanger. "Where's the little bugger?"

I pointed to the weeds. "Is it there?"

"Retreated. Might need teasing out. Stand over there and emphasise your crotch, like," he said.

"Pardon?"

"Little buggers like to snack on cock. Distract him with yours. I'm a cracking shot, lad, you're alright with me," he said. Having cocktucked in time, I was put in the position of having to uncocktuck into the cold wind. I waggle-waggled at violent angles to invite the ravenous elbow towards me, mock-pissing against the Welshman's Daewoo as a form of phallic come-hither. The elbow sprung from the weeds and was blasted mid-spring by the unhoicked shotgun. The corpse landed on the Daewoo bonnet. I peered at the strange mutation close up. It had developed powerful legs and a small head with a set of frightening razor-edged buckteeth, like a pocket-size naked mole rat.

"Dog loves 'em." He retrieved the corpse to feed to his terrier.

"Thanks for the help," I said.

"No problem."

His name was Emrick.

Llanfynydd

'Vertigo: A cod-Fibonacci paean to the Library of Babel' from Barrie Bartmel's *Poems of a Poltroon* (p.43):

> Stunned
> and staggering
> I walk to the entrance
> force open the unoiled doors
> withering under the guardian's glance
> proceed in alphabetic dance to the awaiting A's
> bound to the bountiful B's, cartwheel to the copious C's
> in a bibliophilic swoon I stumble down D to P to T and end at Z
> having poached a dozen from each shelf I prod my barrow
> down towards the scowling guardian for processing
> nose pressed in a volume as she squeaks
> with envy at my freewheeling ways
> and with a thankful glance
> I depart until next week
> for a brand new
> barrowful

Llanfyrnach

Be afraid, Comoros! Icelandic corporate fascism in the warm slippers of liberal democracy is coming!

Llangadog

If I had to sum up Katrin in two words, those words would be "flatulent" and "aloof".

Llangain

Life is timeless. Llangain endless.

Llangattock-Vibon-Avel

No words. (Except those two).

Llangefni

From the parish Twitter: "I urge that Wishy-Washy Wilson drop a nuke on this parish. If he can sack a beadle in 1991, he can sack a priest in 2022. To help the sacking along let me state on the record that I think the Bishop is an incompetent oaf."

Llangernyw

This village houses the oldest tree in Wales, the 4500-year-old Llangernyw Yew. Sadly, there is nowhere in the village to source a passable bowl of custard.

Llangwm

In the surreal haze of the sun, casting an impressionistic light across the River Cleddau, I mused on whether I preferred Stereolab's *Emperor Tomato Ketchup* to *Transient Random-Noise Bursts with Announcements*. As I was about to choose, a rabbit appeared before me, hopping towards shelter with elegance, moving in a such a fleet manner as to render all thoughts of neo-krautrock outfits insignificant.

Llangwnnadl

It is the time of lancing, Rob Dickinson.

Llangwyryfon

Translated, means "the merest hint of verdigris".

Llangybi

Katrin: "I lost my virginity aged fifteen to a fifty-three-year-old plumber in the back of his van. Never forget that."

Llangyhafal

Translated, means "the chicken tikka has been reheated".

Llangyndeyrn

This is what Greg Impasse said to me:

    "Due to extreme fiscal clamping following the pursuit of a long-term career in the writing 'business', I ended up cadging a lift, a boat ride, and accommodation from friends in Orkney in 2009. This was a self-catering cottage for four overlooking the Loch of Hundland, where settlers had carved primitive messages into sandstone (standing for, essentially, fuck foreigners off). I first observed something strange when I checked into the Grisald Guest House, run by the Grisland Brothers. Most of these houses are manned by roseate locals who gambol around in dungarees, or sinister farmhands with nitroglycerine eyes, but the owners of this premises were two long-nosed hunks with chiselled features and Nordic pretensions. From their outward appearance, I had assumed their names Gustav and Olaf—however, Fred and Geoff were their rather disappointing monikers. The Orcadian accent to the untrained ear sounds Welsh as opposed to Nordic. As I unpacked, I thought on the similarity of the noses, and that semicircular crinkle to their lip muscles. They left me their mobile numbers and I went for a swim in the Loch of Hundland in a carked mood."

"Take a breath, Greg."

"Thanks. Swimming round the Loch of Hundland, tossing carp to passing cows, I was surprised when Fred and Geoff bobbed up from the waters to meet me. The brothers, treading water in the centre of the loch, rubbed each others' necks, and kissed passionately as I swam over to say hello. It was too late to retreat, as Fred had clocked me mid-snog, and waved a friendly arm. 'Hey there, Paul! We're having one of our erotic swims. Care for a splish-splash?" Geoff asked. I looked to a carp-munching cow for help. "But you're brothers," I said. Fred chuckled and slapped the water. "Oh, Paul! You've never been to Orkney before, have you? If you had, you would have seen loved-up incestual couplings of sisters and brothers having erotic swims all over the place!" I nodded. Geoff chuckled this time and slapped the water again. "Come to Heldale Water this evening. We're have a traditional sibling orgy, with kissing and heavy petting and apricot sponge. Then we move to Hoglinns Water for full penetration." I passed on their kind offer, and wished them a pleasant collective clasp, causing them to chuckle again and slap the water even harder. They probably considered me tame townie for being uneasy with these casual late-night orgies. In the morning, it made sense to me. Everyone on Orkney was related in one way or another, so making lovers of one's immediate family was merely part of Orcadian tradition. I went along to the next orgy at Heldale, masturbating on moss and having a wonderful time, wishing my sexy cousin was there so I might mount him."

Llanharan

This is what Tjinder Singh said to me:

"I am an Anti-Art Agent (AAA) from the Anti-Art Agency (AAA), hired to further an Anti-Art Agenda (AAA) on behalf of the Anti-Art Authorities (AAA). I am paid £9.50 an hour to sniff out unauthorised creative activity in Llanharan and penalise accordingly. I begin each shift patrolling the village centre, checking the street performers have the correct licenses to sing their songs or strum their instruments or enact their mimes, then pass to the Slum of the Songbird, an ex-industrial estate where writers and artists masquerade as homeless drug-pushers. This liminal zone hosts the largest amount of unauthorised creative activity, with a thousand Fair Deal claimants practicing music, writing, painting, and so on, when they should be looking for full-time work. Our strategies for infiltration have changed over the years. In the past, we would turn up and "storm" these structures, catch the fraudsters in their creative endeavours, and impose immediate penalties on them (the halting of their Fair Deal allowance, or in cases of repeat offence, the instant cancellation of their allowance). Over the years, the artists have become more organised, taking turns to maintain a vigil around each dung-brown windowless crumbling edifice, meaning our presence could be flagged in advance, allowing those practicing unauthorised creative acts inside to hide their pursuits under floorboards, bedclothes, and wall compartments. Since we were not permitted to ransack these premises, we could not find immediate visual evidence, and mete punishment. That morning, I was wearing street clothes and carrying an oboe underarm. It was part of a new initiative to sniff out the covert work-shirkers, to punish them with reasonable cuts, and restore some allowance money into the national budget. I crunched along the gravel, pushed through the overgrown weeds, and sank into a few mudholes before arriving at the entrance of the largest of the three slum buildings (former production lines for the manufacture of washing machines). I rapped on a scarp of sheet metal covering the main entrance. 'Paul Lariat. At work on an oboe concerto,' I said. The metal parted."

Llanhilleth

I remember when I remembered something for the first time. I was six and eating apple strudel in Reykjavik when I remembered kicking my sister in the chin accidentally in the sandpit. "Remember when I kicked you in the chin?" I texted her. That was the first time I remembered remembering something. She remembered.

Llaniestyn

"You are really the most repulsive, soulless, vile-minded person I have ever met. You are a cancerous, spineless, and loveless husk through and through. You are a medieval sewer in female form," I said to Katrin.

Llanishen

Two similar men inhabit two similar homes. This phenomenon is not unusual.

Llanllwch

Fugazi are overrated.

Llanmihangel

'A New Friend' from Barrie Bartmel's *Poems of a Poltroon* (p.16):

> Your explanation
> of the fractious past
> between C3PO
> and R2D2
> is meticulous

And your enthusiasm
for the upcoming
sequel to the prequel
to the forequel to the postquel
is sincere enough

But your words are frozen boulders
falling into the volcanic pools of my ears
And tomorrow I will remember you with some bitterness

Llanmiloe
I am bothered.

Llanover
I would write with Victorian panache on the mythic windswept hills, the scenic coastlines, the ochre sunsets, if this were a travelogue. But it isn't. Plus, I can't write with Victorian panache. So, Bergþórusons, you trusty non-readers of my unending reports, I will continue to write about the pisses I have taken into canoes, tents, and kiosks, and the furtive whackoffings at bikini-clad mothers I have taken as their children played around them. (Relax! I might not have. But I need you to *believe* that I have, and what that says about yourselves for funding this sort of disturbing individual.)

Llanpumsaint
"This is Tale of the Offending Wimple," a pub random said when I asked him to pour nouns into my pinnae. "Once in the 1970s a woman walked out her council flat wearing a wimple. As the favoured headscarf of medieval wenches and nuns, the wimple was not received with rapture among the bus-stoppers or pram-pushers of Llanpumsaint. She entered a shop, purchased a pastry, and upon realising the wimple would attract no comment, returned to her council flat and burned the garment. She would never wear a wimple again."

Llanrhaeadr-ym-Mochnant
A waterfall and the dead.

Llanrhyddlad
Slogan: "Pavements are for losers."

Llanrhystud
Mother, on my sixth birthday: "At some moment, probably around the age of twenty-seven, you will realise that time passes with frightening haste, and that you will become old and pathetic in the blink of an eye, and that you will find yourself backflat in a coffin before you have achieved a single thing of note. You have to pass the time, son. You have to keep busy all the time, or you will tumble into your grave a rotting sack of nothing."

Llanrug
This is what Mac Klonwhip said to me:
    "Listen up, friends and interlopers. In the popular Scottish metropolis of Glasgow, crime fiction had replaced crime as the central preoccupation of the ill-wired. In the era before e-readers, male-ducated miscreants from slum accommodation turned to burglary, arson, stabbing, drug-dealing and sex crime to make the time pass before they became corpses. But what the thugs lacked was imagination. It was simply more of a kick to read about people being murdered in so many unconceivable ways than to attempt original crimes themselves. Likewise, the hard-working ordinary citizens, used to being stabbed or robbed or raped, were not experiencing the same level of criminal interference as before, and needed a replacement fix. Crime fiction was the perfect solution to their problems.
    "Three big names ruled the market until readers realised that crime writers take their inspiration from real-life crimes in the newspapers. It made sense for crime victims to copyright the events that happened to them so crime writers couldn't adapt them for their novels. The reducing crime rate had made the writers' task impossible, and now what little crime there was was being copyrighted before they

could snatch it up. The market was booming but the ideas were no longer there for the taking. There was only one solution. The writers would have to start killing their audience at book signings.

"Jack Richter, one of the three, was the first to strike. He chloroformed his victims and cut off their left arms. His subsequent series, *Armless in Giffnock*, became a number one bestseller. The other two were slower to strike, lacking this author's crazed determination to be the best. Soon, Lorna Doone, the female one, struck blood. She clubbed her victims and removed their feet and teeth. Her subsequent series, *Stand Up Straight & Give Us a Smile*, outsold Richter's series within the first two days. Out of financial desperation, Cal Furnace rose to the occasion and hacked two OAPs to bits in the authors' yurt at the Edinburgh International Book Festival. His series, *Never Too Old to Die*, caused a sensation and made him an instant millionaire. The war raged.

"Richter started stabbing students on campus and dissolving their bodies in acid. Doone took out bankers and businessmen with a silenced pistol in car parks. But Furnace topped them both by strangling newborns in their cots two hours after delivery. It was a move neither Richter nor Doone could have foreseen from the usually timid Furnace. They retired from crime fiction and took up clamming in the Norfolk coast. Meanwhile, audiences were inspired by Furnace's success to try their hand at writing crime fiction in the self-publishing markets. To make sure their writing was authentic, they committed the crimes on the sly and wrote about them as the big names had. Glasgow had returned to the crime-strewn wasteland it had been in the days before e-readers, except each crime was committed in pursuit of literary riches.

"Furnace's days were numbered when Steve McIntosh planned his debut about a killer who takes out a bestselling crime writer by drowning him in a hot tub one night. McIntosh's attempts to snare Furnace was unsuccessful, since Cal had built a ten-foot wall with barbed wire *cheval-de-frise* around his mansion to stop nutters like Steve slipping through. Fortunately, before McIntosh could strike, the British Army invaded Glasgow and blew the city to bits, since military fiction was all the rage in England and retired Colonel Jim Jones was looking for authenticity in his latest bestselling series, *Let's Fuck the Jocks Up With Tanks*. Furnace escaped in a Chinook to Minsk."

Llanstadwell
A retired longshoreman in the pub said to me, in explanation of his unusual choice of tune on the jukebox:

"It is impossible for me listen to Nick Drake. First, the fact that the songs are composed of such aching fragility, timeless mystery, and astonishing beauty, it is almost painful to hear. Second, the fact that the composer of such music of astonishing beauty should resort to suicide because no one listened to or appreciated his albums when he needed the critical encouragement to stabilise his fragile mental state. Third, my own personal misery at the time of hearing these records, and the glum associations I have when listening to them, and the fact the music immediately reminds me of those miserable periods that I would rather forget. It is for these reasons, friend, that I tend to listen to the Sugababes."

Llansteffan
No one in Iceland is working class. Iceland is a series of subtractive colours on a bourgeois bitmap.

Llanthony
"The facially undesirable are the last remaining minority the world is allowed to malign and persecute without recrimination. If all racial and religious prejudice were finished tomorrow, we would still inhabit a world of sideways wincing, of turned backs and sympathetic smirks, of every manoeuvre possible to keep us locked away in basements and attics like mad relatives, out of sight and mind," Katrin moaned.

Llantrisant

There is a plaque here outside the farmhouse where Neil Sedaka once bought asparagus.

Llantrithyd

You are a cunning summit of pus, Robin Guthrie.

Llantwit Major

I met a major twit on land.

"Where does Saddam Hussein keep his biscuits?" he asked.

"Saddam was hanged in 2006," I replied.

"Does he keep them in an old-fashioned circular aluminium tin or in packets in a cupboard or inside packets inside a larger aluminium tin?"

"He was hanged in 2006."

"How many biscuits does he consume in an average 'working' day? Do biscuits form a part of his daily snack strategy at all? Does his erratic dictator's lifestyle eliminate biscuits from his list of necessary eatables?"

"He was hanged."

"Does he restrict himself to red meat and alcohol as a show of masculinity, or does he happily nibble on a custard cream without the slightest worry of appearing effeminate? Does he prefer 'white' biscuits (Rich Teas, Digestives) to 'black' biscuits (Bourbons, Jaffa Cakes)? Is he a biscuit racist?"

"Hanged."

"When he executes somebody for questioning the imperial rightness of his dictatorship, does he like nothing better than a cup of tea and a delicious hobnob? Or does he munch furtively under the covers at night? Does Saddam Hussein's being dead for several years impede his enjoyment of biscuits?"

"I wish you ill," I said, and shoved him into a pedal bin.

Llanvapley
Overheard:

"Before I begin the intended narrative, I must make clear that I suffer from two incurable complexes that make speaking troubling and stressful for me. The first complex, *Digressia Praecox*, renders me prone to tangents and non sequiturs, and a pathological inability to limn a linear narrative. The second complex, *Distractus Distractum*, renders me exceedingly bored by my own words as they hang before me in the air, and liable to completely abandon a sentence or paragraph I am speaking mid-flow, and start another. In attempting to tale this tale, I hope to complete the linear narrative of a man buying a loaf of bread, and thus prove that these complexes are not career impediments."

Llanvihangel Gobion
"Loneliness is the thing," Katrin said.

"What thing?"

"The reason two rotten souls like us remain bound together, even when our faces act as mirrors for how much we loathe ourselves, and loathe each other for reminding us of ourselves, and loathe everyone else for reminding us how their loathing of us makes us loathe ourselves. Loneliness is a busy little brainworm that feeds on the hysterical, paranoid, and self-pitying swill that churns around in one's solitary mind."

Llanwenog
"Why are we even a thing?" Katrin asked. "It isn't you and me versus the world. Whenever my skin mellows into Quantum II mildness, I indulge in scurrilous and unhinged sex with any curved or incurved boycock in the nearby vicinity. The sexual fidelity I have towards you is entirely contingent on dermatological roulette."

Llanybydder
Eastern European slaughterhouse workers and milk.

Llanychlwydog

I have this imagined conversation where I say, "Mother, you are not feminism," and she says, "I am one of the true remaining feminists in the country," and I say, "Your form of loveless Thatcherite feminism is the reason I want to punch feminists," and she says, "No, you want to punch feminists because brute violence has been instilled in you through centuries of Icelandic patriarchy," and I say, "If feminism is never telling your kids you love them then I shit on feminism," and she says, "You resort to scatological imagery when you realise your position as a male is under threat," and I say, "You never loved my father, you are a pseudo-intellectual hagbag, and you probably hate men because you never accepted your true sexuality," and she says, "Sweet Lord, I can't even help you," and I say, "You never tried."

Llanynghendel

First B&B. To save time, it is to be assumed that whenever I meet a stranger, a roster of repulsed and pained looks assault their faces throughout the scene, whether I mention them or not.

Llanyrafon

Overheard:

"All writers should be able to draw a perfect parabola. It is a well-known fact that Rudyard Kipling, Nicholas Royle, Juliet Jacques, Gilvert Sorrismus, and Talcum Iones were able to render perfectly—upon a first try and without consulting the Dictionary of Mathematical Shapes—that splendid curvature known as the parabola. This is how one knows one is in the presence of True Genius. Those talentless pretenders Colm Toibin, Lisa Kerr, Nigel Havers, Harri Matthews, and Bernadette Hoole, upon a first rendering, were only capable of producing an artless hump, such as one might see in a Pacman ghost, or a particularly unsuccessful jellymould. I have always been capable of rendering first-time that remarkable shape, which is why my novels have always reached bestseller status."

Llawhaden
People tell me a bison slept here.

Llay
Yes, I stole 50p from a tramp's cup.

Llyswen
I watch a man lurch across the road, having snorted a line of whatever Popper Pete had perched on his knuckle. I imagine that the drug has tempered with his colour palette, changing reds to greens, blues to browns. He steps across the road, causing a Fiat to swerve into a lamppost, and then a pileup. His sense of reality is speedily booming askew. He steps into a beautiful wonderland, where shards of sensory pleasure flow through his nerve endings, and bliss surges up his body. He approaches a series of pleasurable furry orbs, and rubs his body against them, caressing their wonderful fronds, experiencing the sort of ecstasy usually reserved for private subscribers. He rips his shirt off, drops to his knees, feverishly licking the orbs, chasing the ones that are darting around the room. After two minutes, he feels a violent tugging and suddenly loses consciousness. His manuscript is bloodied as the ambulance arrives in the school playground, where he was licking the childrens' heads. The paramedics note with disgust that he is erect. It is Bob Driscoll. Nicolas Lezard called his first novel "a blast of fresh air in a stifling fiction market."

Longmoor
Promenades and avenues. Longmoor endless.

Ludchurch
I swear I saw the staggered apparition of William H. Macy coming over the hill.

Lydstep Haven
Helga Horsedóttir, for you, I would help a fumbling elder secure her parsnips.

Maenaddfwyn

"Perseverance pays off," a man told his son.

"Excuse me," I stepped in. "This is parent-speak for 'Even if you pass your A-Levels, succeed at university, and enter a preferred career, the slow inevitable touch of despair, ennui, and self-hatred will eventually smother your spirits.'"

I was not punched.

Maerdy

"I spit on Adrian Hasler," a spindly man said.

Maeshafn

Sometimes I worry when I am spooning gelato into my maw that I have never had an actual thought in my life, that I have merely been coasting along on some panglobal thought-wave, parroting the soulless tripe of billions, and that any deviation from this tripe would see me banished to a skull-caked dungeon in Addis Ababa, where originality has been starved to death for millennia by the cunts who keep us stupid.

Maesteg

I stand by nothing I have written in these "reports". Whatever is written is valid at the moment of writing and represents nothing more than the short process of thoughtlessness that took place between expression of the first and last words. If I re-read anything I wrote I would probably seek to run myself through with a longsword. (As I am sure you are seeking to do, Bergþórusons, if I flatter myself you are reading).

Maesycwmmer

I am the purblind simpleton of the Urals.

Maindee

It is not an untrue statement that I spent an hour and thirty-seven minutes in an inviolable cuddle with Helga's Facebook.

Mamhilad

I wish there was somewhere nearby to source fresh tomatoes, potatoes, or asparagus.

Manafon

I read about a man who leapt in front of a truck to save a toddler from a fatal splatting. He was paralysed for life, and in his hospital bed, having first heard the news of his condition, asked first if the child was all right. It was a humbling moment of absolute selflessness. Then I remembered the songs of Keane. My pleasure was pulped to a wet, shapeless mass.

Mancot

If this village were a lament of the short-sighted, it would be that recurring smudge on the right lens that never seems to smudge off.

Manordeilo

Sometimes the afternoon is leased to an opioid-lover with a crunched sternum.

Manorowen

Helga, here are five things I would do to secure a flecklet of your ardour:
1. Depend on the dull.
2. Lick lichen in Liechtenstein.
3. Consider an inappropriate marriage to an Anglo-Venusian solicitor.
4. Brainwash a creche.
5. Take a ruminant and relax.

Marian Glas

The Quantum Scale of Facial Catastrophes (in five phases):

Quantum 3—"The Full Quasimodo": You exist in a nail-biting realm of unpredictable facial pandemonium, where spontaneous volcanic upbumpings will appear without warning on places where prior upbumpings had cleared or had never upbumped. You will experience hideous and unpoppable bumps the morning of important life moments—your bat mitzvah, your confirmation day, your fourth marriage—causing the people around you to seriously consider the social consequences of being around you, as your oily skin weeps pus and your red scabby pockets lightly bleed.

Melin-y-Coed
Moving further into mutation country, crossbow in tow. The automatic pistol I ordered from the Dark Net never arrived at the B&B, after two weeks waiting. I had to move on. As I drove further into the meltdown radius, more oddities appeared. A common sight were flaming sheep unbothered at the fact of their flamingness, lazing and nibbling as usual without a second thought to their burning coats. I stopped to inspect one stuck in a fence. The illusion of this flamingness was a consequence of the malcogens, merging to form a reddish-amber hologram of flames around the fur, a strange invisible blanket of fake burning with a notable whiff of asphalt. Further on up the road, other illusions appeared, including sheep encased in a thick ice, sheep that appeared to be levitating, and sheep encased in rainbows. These oddities added a pleasant aspect to the cut-and-paste rurality of Snowdonia.

Meline
'I Have Seen' from Barrie Bartmel's *Poems of a Poltroon* (p.13):

> I have seen the sheds of Egypt
> and Brian Wilson's Twitter feed
>
> and I have seen the last ever waltz
> and a bowlful of cement
>
> But I decree
>
> there is nothing better
> than rapping on a woman's door
> waiting for that door to open

and after seeking her permission
kissing her on the face
and then kissing her
on her face
twice
and twice again
and twice
again

Merthyr Mawr

I am lying naked and erect on Helga's lavender-scented king-size bed. From the bathroom she emerges in a white suspender belt, stockings, and a lace bodice. The tip of her pale white breasts poke from the small shell-like cups saying, "Hello! I am yours." She sultries towards the bed and takes me in her mouth. I lie back and watch her ink-blank ringlets curl upon my belly. I stroke her hair as her tongue caresses the shaft, her little lips planting kisses on the tip before her mouth closes round again. I am the recipient of unadulterated sexual bliss. I would not leave this room for a trillion shekels. I lie back and sink into the swirling stucco pattern overhead. When I look down I observe that Helga has removed her head from her body and is stood in the corner in a Knattspyrnufélagið Valur FC strip. She limbers up and takes a kick at her head and my penis, booting both out the window. Not for the first time in an erotic reverie, I am cockless and bleeding. I wake up in a sticky tumult.

Minffordd

Y lle hwn yn rhywiol!

Minwear

Be afraid, Djibouti! Icelandic corporate fascism in the warm slippers of liberal democracy is coming!

Mitcheltroy Common

It helps to imagine Helga Horsedóttir looks like this:

Mochdre

Pauletta Crouther, the Orcadian, said to me:

"I run the finest Orkney Library & Archive in Conwy. Our new releases: *From South Ronaldsay to Papa Westray: Orkney's Most Thrilling Stones*; *Ye Missed The Ba'!: The Funniest Fatalities in Orkney's National Game*; *Big Book of Orcadian Farmer Fashions*; *Mummy, Where are All the Trees?: How to Explain Orkney's Arboreal Shortage to Your Children*; *Lay Back and Stay Calm: What to Do in the Event of a Perverted Landlord*; *Magnus or Thorfin?: Choosing Your Baby's Name*; *George Mackay Brown: The Only Writer to Ever Come from Orkney*; *OMG! I Love Dounby SO MUCH!: Tourist's Guide to Coping with Your Overwhelming Excitement*; *Orkney: Home of Australasian Erotic Pottery*; *Not Just a Bunch of Smelly Farmers: Complete Guide to the Landed Gentry Living on the Island*; *Handbook on Westray's Thriving Gay Scene*; *Mine Howe Ye Go!: Illustrated Guide to Descending the Steps*; *Is That Your Cock, Sir?:A Proud History of Orcadian Orgies*. All published in hardcover from GMB Books Ltd."

Mold

This is what Brian Gongo said to me:

"I met C. Matthews at a campsite in 1995. Her pomo-rock number Catatonia had released their *Hooked* EP two months prior, and 'Cariadon Ffôl' had appeared on the *S4C Makes Me Wanna Smoke Crack* showcase, a piquant EP of taff-pop. I was an appreciator. 'Those stoned licks evoke the chamber-pop of The 13th Floor,' I said to impress. C. was not amused although I managed to sneak a phone number into her coat pocket. I started making whoopee with her around the release of 'Bleed', the first single from *Way Beyond Blue*. The tour was a mild bacchanal of nicotine and the hand-stitched zines of Brian Salter, model village obsessive. In the bus, we would spend hours reading the opinions on micro Yorks, Charlburys, and Hebden Bridges as we blitzed two packs of B&H. These were the fondest times in our twosome. Then came the trainwreck of 'Murder & Scully', and the explosion of *International Velvet*. As this classic Britpop single shot up the charts, C. had taken up model villaging as a pastime, working on her own nano-rendering of the North Wales seaside perennial Llandudno. She created a replica the size of a coffeetable, and added realistic detail such as actual shop signs, railings, and the resigned expressions of the inhabitants. As ladette indie erupted in the British pop rags, with the likes of Elastica and Sleeper, C. made a show of similar loutish extravagance, while in secret she was entrenched in her painstaking replica of Llandudno.

"As these were pre-internet times, C. insisted we take impromptu trips to Llandudno for architectural research, and she spent hours taking photos of cornices and walls and awnings. Back on the bus, she would add microscopic detail to various shops, including likenesses of known shop owners standing at the windows. These trips sometimes involved three-hour drives. One time, we were heading to a concert in Aberdeen when she began working on the attractions at the pier, and had not been able to source photographs. 'Screw the show! I need to get to Llandudno!' she shouted, ramming open the tour bus door and threatening to leap out. We had to cancel the concert and drive 400 miles back to Wales. This obsession continued as the tour progressed. C. was able to turn on the ladette whenever appearing on chat shows like TFI Friday or Live & Kicking. When the cameras stopped she leapt back into dungarees to replicate the fire damage to the B&B on Madoc Street. The rest of the band launched themselves into the hedonistic life, taking coked-up groupies to the tour bus, and having loud romps. I sat in the back of the bus with C. reading the novels of Sinclair Lewis and keeping as shtum as I could without breaking her immense concentration. I tried to tempt her with a bag of cocaine. I encouraged her to sleep with male groupies. Nothing except model villages had pull.

"For the entire *International Velvet* tour, the height of Catatonia's pop-cult prominence, she split her personalities in twain. The cracks showed on the last performances in Belgrade and Munich when she was seen on stage considering whether the porticoes on the town hall were Doric or Edwardian. This was written on her face, and the audiences responded with boos. As she launched into an encore rendition of 'Road Rage', the crowd were moved to heckle as her singing revealed her trepidation on running out of matchsticks to complete the pier. Back home in Cardiff, C. bought a house with a hectare of land and began work on a model village version of Prestatyn. Our relationship mellowed somewhat, as C. spent more time acknowledging I existed in between her monomaniacal pursuit. The band had completed the music for the follow-up album, *Equally Cursed & Blessed*, in September 1998, although C. had zero interest in writing. I had to imitate her waspish wit as I wrote most of the words for that LP ("high-street prams chariot scene from Ben-Hur pushchair rage" was a particular nadir), as C. spent her 1998-1999 completing her enormous replica of Prestatyn until she frittered her funds. She sprung into the studio at once and the album was cut in a week. A mix of swishing ballads ('Nothing Hurts') and sardonic filler ('Storm the Palace'), *EC&B* is a sweet ragbag.

"The tour for this record was a nightmare. I was asked to remain at home and oversee minor improvements on the village such as the buttresses at the bingo hall which required additional caulking, and the local schools which needed asbestos in their ceilings. The entire tour I spent on a live link-up with C., using the lame webcam tech at the time, having to zoom in so she could see a pixelated imitation of her work so far. 'Lower. Lower. To the right. Lower,' she said, on and on and on. We would snap at each other if I was seen to be tampering with her work (I offered to help to her strong refusal). The band rushed her into the studio at the end of the tour to cut the execrable *Scissors Paper Stone*, a rotten postscript to their short time as the flaming meteors of Welsh indie. C. returned to her model village and over the next three years, worked on her Prestatyn with obsessive precision. I broke with her in 2002, when she had taken to hurling insults at her helpers. I had become a helper at this stage—I tried to kiss her once, and she recoiled and ordered me to fetch the cement.

"In 2003, she showcased her completed model at the Model Village Show in LA and won Best of Britain. After, she went into rehab and wrote a set of songs that became her solo LP *Cockahoop*. She sent me a letter apologising for her behaviour some months later. It is a shame that C. was unable to relish in her success. Such a large number of people take to making model villages at a perilously young age. It is a much misunderstood addiction. I am proud that C. is now an ambassador for the organisation that supports the rehabilitation of those in need, Model Village Erectors Anonymous."

Monachty
The people here want fewer sheep.

Monington
The people here want an undefinable unachievable something that tastes like chocolate and salves the pain of being alive. In fact, the people here want chocolate.

Monknash

'Kissing Melanie' from Barrie Bartmel's *Poems of a Poltroon* (p.13):

> You were a plump schoolteacher
> from Penyrheol
> and I kissed you one November evening
> after a screening of *Philomena*
> at the Swansea Odeon
> after two minutes of stammering
> your permission sought
> and your chapsticked lips
> met my chapped ones
> as I took more than my allotted share
> of snog-time
> from your tolerant mouth
> and I bade you farewell
> to catch my train
> where I was too excited to read my novel
> (Federman's *Double or Nothing*)
> and remained blissfully unaware
> of the polite see-you-around text the next morning
> denying me the pleasure of seeing your plump
> Penyrheol body
> in a bed somewhere
> in that small flat you said you had
> somewhere over there
> behind that pub

Monkswood

Translated, means "letted cottage in tarnished amber".

Moriah

Katrin said: "I encouraged my father's adultery. I told him, 'Dr. Alice Verdance, sexpert at Harvard, wrote that marriages built on a solid bedrock of extramarital affairs are the happiest ones. Your wife has probably taken several dozen lovers, so to keep your marriage in tip-top shape, you should have sex with Martha Ketteridge.' "

Morvil

I put a soil sample in a vial.

Moss Valley

You will weep on the pillow tonight, Yuki Chikudate.

Mountain Ash

A hitchhiking man appeared on a road.

"Hello sir," I started. "How is your wife?"

"She has, inexplicably, traitorously, become rabidly in favour of harvesting a foetus. I explained to her that the population of the world will approximate 9.77 billion in 2050, in an era when we will hack each other to pieces for a can of petrol. And she said that her womb cried out for the kick inside, to quote Kate Bush."

"That's awful."

"She will not let the statistics sit in the way of her craving for a mewling flesh-blob. I say, look, the world population by 2100 will be 11.2 billion, and she says, no matter, I want a wee bald babykins. I say, look, over 1 billion children worldwide are living in poverty, and in sub-Saharan Africa children under 5 die from easily treatable diseases, and she says, no matter, I want a poop-nappy. I say, the concentration of particulate pollution is rising and the pro-fossil fuel lobbies are winning, and she says, no matter, I want to tickle ickle toes. I say, nearly half the world's population live on less than £1.97 per day, and the 1% wealth-hoarders want more and she says, no matter, I want to kiss that doughy forehead. Our future is shaky."

"Strange."

"She used to subscribe to Baumgardener's third-wave feminist notion that mothers were scorned by society, that the Gen-X woman had been sacrificed at the altar of sprog-wiping."

"Hmm."

"She feared the slackening of her sexual prowess, the loosening of her pelvic muscles, and the real threat of haemorrhoids."

"Hmm."

"She feared that she would loathe her child, and that in loathing her child she would come to loathe me, and that she would ultimately loathe herself, and that she would spin off into madness and misery."

"Hmm."

"Then one evening she wanted to be inseminated."

"Pfffffftttt."

"Is the correct noise to make."

"Get out of my car."

Mounton

Trimming excess testicular hair in the Saab, Lucinda Williams blasting hard on the stereo.

Myddfai

You cannot be a misanthrope until you have spent twelve minutes mopping up the excess pus from a hellburst anal wart.

Mydroilyn

Man. Pub. Evening.

"Have you heard rumours round the frictious depictions in Nicola's fictions?" man asked.

"Lager," I said, pointing to glass.

"There have been claims that Nicola's fictions have increased the level of ill-concealed malice against certain persons in her real life. Ferdinand Apple, former landlord of Nicola's during her time in Enniskillen, received a cruel caricaturing in her latest story, where he appears as a parsnip-nosed loan shark named Goo who slaps a snoring child while collecting overdue rent from its rakehell father. 'This is an inaccurate me. I believed Nicola to be respectful to the people she sketches in her fiction,' Ferdinand said. He was seen weeping in a coffee shop a few hours later over a cold latte. Another real person, Terrance Onion, worked with Nicola during her temping years in Thurso, and was included in the first chapter of her novel as a squat loner in a knitted sweater eating microwave noodles over Xmas. 'I have never worn such inadequate knitwear, nor eaten cheap meals,'

Terrance said. He was seen consulting his GP about a new-formed depression two hours later. Several thousand similar claims have sprung up. A council bureau investigating the harmful sting in Nicola's fictions has been set up, spearheaded by Marcus Openhair, who clamped down on the excessive reindeer descriptions in Norman's fictions two years earlier, causing a reduction in the demand for reindeer meat. The bureau will examine the direct link between suicidal thoughts, severe depression, and public weeping outbursts, and the cruelness of Nicola's obvious depictions of real life people. If the situation is not resolved after the investigation has been concluded, the bureau might be forced into writing an email to Nicola, asking her to pen milder depictions in future fictions."

"Oh," I said. "Lager."

Mynydd Cerrig
I tend to nap around 12.30. I wake up spine-burgled and tarnished.

Mynydd Isa
Home to Wales's finest Four Tet tribute act.

Mynyddislwyn
Mother: "In your heart is a happy smiling man. He bombs around the pavement with a shit-eating grin, as though in possession of a winning lottery ticket. In twelve minutes' time, that man will be slowly crushed under the wheels of an ice-cream truck."

Mynytho
This is what Michael Clem said to me:

"And what a delirious time I had with Petra Kant in the eclipse of our beginning. 'You must be a man of monumental arrogance to believe that your writing deserves to be read. That your interpretation of human interactions will offer the reader the faintest insight into the nature or meaning of existence,' she said during our first writers' tête-à-tête, and I rebutted with loving sallies suggesting that if a writer can move only one person in a lifetime then their striving has not been in vain. She was working on a Beckett-like tale concerning a homeless woman raiding trash cans for sentences to incorporate into her own speech so she might stumble upon something meaningful and thus move another human being to a state of happiness or pain or fear. I forged ahead with the novel about the impact a school bus crash had on a small mining town, summoning up the enormous thicket of grief and loss in this desolate place and searching for hope amid the despair as Petra poured into my ear: 'There's no place for the sham feeling in fiction . . . all we do as writers is scrabble around in trash dump of precooked language looking for scraps of cold emotion to serve up as our own.' This despair about existing in a post-linguistic age where no words are sufficient conveyors of feeling erected an enormous barrier for our prosaic everyday love relationship. I was forced to examine the sincerity behind each gesture of affection and soon came to loathe the flip I-love-you, rolled off the tongue and served cold into a blasé heart used to the swift dissolving of such stale offerings. I pulled away from Petra as the villagers dammed up their tears in favour of long contemplation of the existential void that was human life without distractions like children and marriages, and likewise I sank into the fearful silence that was our relationship, frightened that a simple touch on the shoulders or whispered compliment would be absorbed into the trash heap along with those other meaningless words."

Nannerch
Here, catladies bark nouns into mounds of brick and mortar while seeking in vain for the periscopic paw of their crushed mogs.

Nant-y-Moel
Translated, means "she was scrubbed auburn".

Nantglyn
"I just thought well fuck it man, I'm gonna pack my soul and scram," I heard Iggy sing.

Nantmor
Nibbling brie on the A4085. Cheese, I salute thee.

Nantycaws
Sometimes I am too repulsed with myself to sit up. So I don't.

Nantyglo
I loathe writing with a "purpose" or a "message", writing that makes "points", or has "consistency." How vainly these plodding hacks strive to knit meaning from the tumbling yarn of chaos, and luxuriate in their positions as eminent figure-outers. I am more interested in profoundly confusing the reader, in pouring a form of intellectual distortion into their heads, like a prose version of skronk. It is the writer's business to feed the reader a banquet of falsehoods. Our lives are an unnavigable series of unstable narratives careering into a vast postmodern soup of unknowing. We wrap ourselves in lies, frantically masturbate into their intoxicating wrongness, and sink sated into our duvets of delusion. It's what we like.

Narberth
As I pass into middle age, I come closer to accepting that life consists of little except the constant abatement of sexual desire, killing time with futile, transient and shallow activity, and fearing death while secretly willing it nearer.

Nefyn
I am crying in my Saab, sucking on a mango.

Nelson
Eating a taco when I recalled Iggy Pop shirtless in a British advert saying, "I'm not selling car insurance, I'm selling time," to which every betrayed viewer in the world replied, "No, you asscamel, you're selling car insurance".

Nevern

There were rumours that one of Katrin's exes committed suicide following her ruthless discarding and that she celebrated with a £30 bottle of champagne and a trip to the sauna. Someone told me that in Grindavik.

New Brighton

If the perpetual and pointless longing I have for a raven-haired Icelandic woman in her early thirties with a five-year-old daughter were a sound, and that sound was encapsulated in a Glaswegian twee-pop unit, that sound would be the complete works of Camera Obscura.

Newbridge-on-Usk

Splendour and overpriced prawn cocktail.

Newbridge-on-Wye

I bumped into the Scottish man who loathed crime writer Ian Rankin.

"Last time we met, I was explaining my loathing of the crime writer Ian Rankin," he recapped.

"Oh."

"I have envied Ian Rankin since the first poke of awareness of his existence morphed into a multi-limbed grope of awareness of his existence and stature and fame and first name: Ian. His kindly face insinuated itself into my consciousness like that recurring nightmare where a plump man in a mink coat pursues my naked six-year-old body through seventeen corridors while humming 'Leaning on the Everlasting Arms'. The novels of Ian Rankin partypooped their way into my perception in my late teens, first seen in their scores in second-hand bookshops, where the Inspector Rebus series provides a form of additional cavity wall insulation and an ersatz caulking to absorb encroaching damp. His novels are, quite literally, keeping Scottish second-hand bookshops from crumbling."

"Ha."

"I was raised, like Rankin, in an inconsequential village in the lower half of Scotland's low-hanging breeks, in a working-class prefab where "possibility" was a word that had long been riddled with bullets and buried in a landfill. Like Rankin, I attended The University of Edinburgh, where I studied literature. Like Rankin, I have a repulsive haircut and a beauty spot on my right cheek (his is, of course, larger). Like Rankin, I was a punk musician in a band named The Dancing Pigs (left-handed slap-bass, occasional bongo duties). And like Rankin, I was a striving and ambitious writer, whose first few books were literary novels (although mine are better). Then our paths and personalities diverged."

"No kidding."

"Rankin is a sociable, loveable, street-smart renaissance man rammed too far up the hindgut of Scottish culture to ignore. I am a hermit-like, unlovable, woodland-dwelling one-trick wonder who never participates in Scottish culture apart from attending the Glasgow Film Theatre to watch Russian miserablism. Rankin is a man who wears his Scottishness with ease, penning essays on whisky and not living in London. I wear my Scottishness like a damp undershirt two sizes two small, penning tomes where Scotland is blown to smithers in a merciless nuclear attack from Luxembourg. Rankin likes hip new indie bands and reads comics. I like early-80s Shonen Knife and the novels of Rodrigo Fresán. Rankin is an OBE and FRSE. I will never receive these honours, as I will never be populist enough. Rankin has no complex about writing popular genre fiction for a broad audience while maintaining a sideline in cool countercultural activities that endear him to most unembittered people. I resent writers who write for an audience and spend most of my time indulging my niche interests that no one particularly likes and pretending not to care. Rankin had an extramarital affair, cultivating a "bad boy" persona. I have no capacity for romantic betrayal and I find myself riddled with shame for masturbating to another woman's breasts. Rankin is a millionaire with a large Edinburgh mansion and eats lobster bisque. I have no money and live in a third-floor flat and eat Wotsits. Rankin is everything I could have been, if I had veered another way, if I had hoed another road, if I had been born Ian Rankin. As a consequence, I observe him in motion across the Scottish literary orrery, moving like an fast-flaming meteorite towards the darkened moon of my pointless ambition. He is my destroyer. He is my nemesis. He is the living physical embodiment of everything I loathe about Scotland and Scottish literature."

"Have you read any of the Rebus novels?"

"Now that *is* chucklesome."

"Then your discourse is valueless."

"I had a 'look inside' at one on Amazon. It has this sentence: 'She seemed to have given up the steak and was dabbing her mouth with her napkin.' "

"And?"

"If that is literature, Allan Massie, I might as well pack in the whole thing. And the other sentences ain't shining timeless beacons neither."

"Who's Allan Massie?"

"He's coming up."

"Look, mein Freund, have you made a comprehensive study of Scottish crime fiction for this discourse? That is all I care about. I am sitting here thinking 'if he hasn't researched this, his opinions are meaningless, this discourse is a waste of my time, and this discourse, critically, has no aesthetic or academic value, and what we expect from our modern writers is a basic level of immersiveness, so we can praise their hard-won words that spill from their fact-packed brains to the page to our empty, factless brains.' That is what I think. I won't accept a single word of this vacuous critique unless you have immersed yourself in the works of thirty-six crime novelists, and read the entire works of Rankin twice."

"In this discourse, I have scrunched the concept of 'reasoned analysis' into a spiteful ball and hurled that ball towards a flaming bin, much like I do when I read another four-star Rankin review in a broadsheet. I tear the page from that paper, observing phrases like 'much-loved detective' and 'atmosphere as rich as the plot', and lunge them towards the unopened window in a fuming whirl of frothing hatred, only to have the pages bounce back towards my crying face, and brush my lips, as if the author is trying to seduce me through the stabby crunch of his scrunched-up broadsheet review. This discourse is an intense probing of and unconcise lancing of a yam-yellow literary boil. That yam-yellow boil is named Ian Rankin."

"I have to leave again."

"I still haven't finished."

"Diddums."

Newcastle Emlyn

A couple emerged from a cinema, in all probability, having seen a film that mirrored some of the exact rituals of their courtship. Stepping into the street, the rain began to fall, echoing a scene where the protagonists emerge from a cinema, and the man remembered he loved the woman somewhat. His attempt to reach over and take her hand is interrupted by: "Look! It's raining like in the film! Funny that!" He remembered precisely why he only loved her somewhat.

Newchurch

I tongue-kissed the air for seven seconds in an apse.

Newtown

Farted with a vengeance in Morrisons.

Neyland

A father strolls along the street rebuffing his toddler's hand, allowing the toddler to lag behind. It is as if the father is pretending the toddler is not with him.

Oakenholt

There is a plaque here outside the post office where Aleks Krotoski once mailed a threatening letter.

Oakford

A rogue elbow bruised Katrin's clavicle.

Ogmore

I stared at a bowheaded teen at a bus stop and attempted a mental sketch of his lot. There are times when he's feeling awful—and by "feeling" he means how his brain and body responds to the never-changing rigours of life, i.e. he'll know he's "feeling" low because he is categorically incapable of thinking a single rational thought, and his whole body moves like blancmange—and times when he's "feeling" not so awful, but still basically awful, though not awful enough to collapse into apathy. There's an important distinction between what's he's "feeling" inside and what he's "feeling" on public record. When his parents ask him every morning "how he's feeling," he spares them the early morning melancholy by not telling them over their toast and eggs that he still basically "feels" worthless, i.e. that his brain keeps telling him there is no place for him in the world, and if there were a place for him in the world, surely after seventeen years of life he might have intimated this by now, and he still can barely bring himself to wobble out of bed and face the day. Instead, every morning, he is "all right," two hopeful syllables grunted inaudibly to convince himself that he is in fact "all right," and that the last two years of thickening fog were simply some macabre special effect. So his parents, as they leave for work, as they drive him to the station, can focus on their days without taking the unrelenting sadness of their child with them to work, which would make them, in turn, "feel" bad about themselves (though to what degree his parents "felt" his misery he couldn't know, as they could only offer him the same old solutions—why don't you go to the doctor? you ought to go out and meet people, son—and so on, knowing his unbearable crippling shyness made him physically unable to even open the door, let alone find these "people" that would magically make his life worth living). And so he was incapable of feeling without inverted commas, because all he ever did daily was feel, feeling the same loneliness, self-hatred and depression that seemed to negate the act of "feeling" completely and spray it with this gauzy block, this mist in his vision, where he could see nothing except the sad little teenager in his poky little bedroom, trying so hard to be like everyone else his age, walking and talking and laughing and feeling nothing but the bliss of being young and in love with a world of unlimited possibilities, not having to worry about whether he could feel anything anymore except oblivion, or whether to count his feelings as feelings or "feelings," as tangible emotions to be acknowledged, or ugly obstacles to be blasted into outer space so he could get out there and touch a girl's breast, drink a delicious beer, or do whatever normal people did.

Ogmore Vale
Is it worse to have a blissful childhood and an adulthood spent pining for those carefree times, or a miserable childhood and an adulthood spent pining for a carefree childhood that never existed?

Old Colwyn
Stabbings and casual racism.

Oldcastle
'Congratulating You' from Barrie Bartmel's *Poems of a Poltroon* (p.29):

> Finding the words
> to praise your achievements
> as I sit here in my pants eating pâté
> is a task
> for which the term Herculean
> is insufficient
>
> "Your success is well-earned," I try,
> meaning not a single word.
> "I am so pleased for you," I try,
> meaning not a single word.
> "Whoo-hoo! Amazing!" I cry,
> meaning not a single word.
>
> So instead I write "congrats!"
> and will never speak to you again
> until I too am seeking a chance to

flaunt my achievements among
indifferent figures from my past
from whom I wished to be
insincerely congratulated

Pant

"You see in Helga a strong and independent woman who will never care for you no matter what you do," Katrin explained. "All your adolescent lusting over this woman is a failed campaign to delude yourself that your mother loved you."

Pantasaph

Another lunatic in a cagoule accosting me outside the WC.

"Morning!" he bellowed. I replied not.

"Morning!" he rebellowed and curved towards me.

"Morning! I am the narrator in a story no one will ever read. You might think—oops, little slip there—*I* might think that is liberating. To be able to say anything without fear of adverse reactions from sensitive, fussy readers. But it isn't. It's constraining. I can't write to impress anyone, and if I can't impress anyone, or impact another person at all in any minor way, then why write—or live—at all? So I realise the only solution is to kill myself. That is, my story self. The person writing this story will only 'die' when the story ends. But how does one narrate one's own suicide? I can't write 'I slit my throat' because . . . I see the dilemma. So all I can say is, I have a gun in my left hand, I'm pointing it at my head. (Of course, I could write a fictionalised approximation of how the event might go but why would I want to do a stupid thing like that?) At the end of this sentence I will have 'blown my brains out', as the phrase goes."

I replied not.

Panteg

I am slurping banana milk when I recall the scene from Aku Louhimes's *Frozen Land* when an alcoholic salesman murders a man and a woman in the act of coitus using a vacuum cleaner. It is upsetting how often I consider that scene whenever I am at a wedding.

Pantside
The people here want an end to the cruel insinuations of stewards.

Pantyresk
From the parish Twitter: "I urge the Diocesan Big Cheese to shut up this shop. No punters here, chaps. I am literally addressing empty pews every Sunday, and while I respect wood in all its lignifications, the collection plate is rarely filled."

Paradwys
Alanis Morrissette, like the flame-tongued Liz Phair, was unable to harness happiness for artistic supremacy. The insipid roster of records that followed in the wake of *Jagged Little Pill* is proof that one youthful heart-pounding creamed the artist's talents entire, with later lapses into love and contentment tempering the tuneful tantrums that made her third LP such a pleasant hour of hellcat ear-shriek.

Pemberton
I am ramfeezled.

Pembrey
Parks, hotels, and palaces. Pembrey endless.

Pen-y-clawdd
The people here want more sheep.

Pen-y-waun
A familiar daydream. On returning to work, a kind of shuddery brio invades my body. People look me with expressions that say "Precisely what is that man of facial integrity doing over there in that cupboard?" Men step down from desks and say, "Let me see you," and stroke my cheek. I felt emboldened enough in the thought-node to say, "Excuse me, but shouldn't our notions be buffed to a thermal sheen?" Max

Bergþóruson widens his lips to an 'O' into which one might insert a salami. I note the circumference of the 'O' and know this denotes impressedness. "Yes, I suppose they should," he says. The room goes "Woow!" I then push my luck. "And, following on from that unravelling of now, let me add, that the worst kind of preponderance is the velcro." The room erupts into applause. There are hoots, toots, and whoops. One man faints. Max approaches me for a full kiss on the mouth and tickles my balls. The sunshine eats my face.

Pen-y-wenallt
Translated, means: "Beneath the bleak Ceredigion clouds, a collection of spindleshanked mammals with hair and teeth circumnavigate the parlous nation of their navels. A sprinkling of warmblooded bonebags stride along the crux of chaos, across asphalt and cobbles and mud and puddles, sucking in a scare of icecold Cambrian air, towards the impossible plop of their circs. These Williams and Stevens and Carols and Nicolas, those Andrews and Damons and Fionas and Henriettas, them Olivers and Reginalds and Karens and Claires, swallowing fourteen pints of saliva per lunar phase, ill-at-ease in their awkward bodies, teeter towards brick structures with shower nozzles and Apple Macs and swivel chairs and curtains, populating a topless topos on the verge of toppling. Opening their sleep-encrusted peepers to this unstated burp of time, in a fictive rendering of the unreal running verso to recto, the inhabitants of an austere port city awake with alarm, bumble from their beds, crawl from their cots, dangle from their duvets, exit their erotic escapades, fumble for their formerselves, grope their gorgeous genitals, howl for help, inclick their inboxes, jog in their jodhpurs, lick their lovers' limbs, mumble at their mums, nix their nosehairs, opine their odious opinions, prod their porky partners, quibble over quilts, read random reports, spruce their sprogs, tend to their teeth, un-undress their underparts, vroom to their vehicles, wobble to their workplaces, X-out their x-pectations, yearn for yesterday, and zip to their zerohoods. A clocktower, looming over the piss-wet plaza, points accusing arrows of time at the watching watchless, and the re-

liable rain soaks stone for the ninth time that hour as skittering persons uneager to sit with sodden pates flock from the clock. Strings of coughing cars pour along lined strips, taking Iains and Percys, Mirandas and Mollys, to their temporary storage cupboards, revving and purring in the rain like frisky, hellacious cats. And as time's maw inches open another cruel millimetre, these ragbag entities, in their coats and shirts and skirts and corsets, lunge towards lunchtime with the springiness of a Devonshire rabbit, appraising their apples, bothering their broccoli, cooling their custard, downing their dumplings, eviscerating their eclairs, forking their fusilli, gargling their gingerbeers, hacking their hamhock, inverting their incaberries, jactitating their jalapenos, knifing their kokam, lancing their lambshanks, mauling their mascarpone, nibbling their nutterbutters, O-mouthing their olives, pecking their parrotfish, quickchewing their quesadillas, ruining their rhubarbtarts, swallowing their swordfish, tuttuting at their taramasalata, undoing their uunijuusto, vivisecting their viennasuasages, x-ing their xocolatl, yumyumming their yuzu, zapping their zucchinis. Toil pummels these mindless invertebrates around the arms and arse. The burning fingers of commerce creep along their necks, pressing their windpipes with a hostile 'Hi!', causing a slow chokehold as the clock remains locked in smug immovability, tocking and never ticking and ticking and never tocking."

Pen-yr-hoel
DREAM [33]: I am eating pizza in the cramped campbed in my rickety shed. Every slice tastes like the inviolate portals of your charm.

Penally
Be afraid, Guyana! Icelandic corporate fascism in the warm slippers of liberal democracy is coming!

Pencoed
I met Katrin the sixth time in my apartment. She recommended reverse cowgirl to prevent mutual vomitus.

Pendoylan

I have been picturing Helga Horsedóttir as this chap for so long I am struggling to muster up workable boners.

Penffordd

Overheard:

"Peter, I have written on this issue prior in *New Opinions Issue 4*. These points need no reiteration. The statement I wrote on Burroughs was re-echoed in *The Beast Magazine* and championed in *The Truncheon*. You were reading *Naked Lunch* when the statement was being printed and this had no bearing on your response to the novel. We discussed this at Grandma's (she had read *Queer* in the 1950s and made no comment). This issue is stale. I am bored repeating the well-worn opinions I have voiced in public and have no intention of doing so here. You can purchase these back issues and contact me when an intelligent riposte occurs to you. I live in San Andreas at the moment and have visitors. Please do not mail me that first hardback edition of *Interzone*. I will not accept this as a present."

Pengam

I met Katrin the fifth time at a screening of *Margin Call*. She put her hand on my penis for an hour and two minutes. This went unremarked.

Pengorffwysfa

Slogan: "So much more than a closed Calvinist chapel."

Peniel

I took it upon myself to contradict myself. There is a pleasure, Bergþórusons, in loosing oneself from the snug pelt of your shrink-wrapped opinions, and volte-faceing your merry way into a shrieking cavern of lies.

Penllwyn

Having a rancid feminist for a mother might have made me loathe the proper, unrancid feminists and the movement itself. Not so. If there were more proper, unrancid feminists around, my mother would no longer have a platform.

Penmaenmawr

A creep in a blazer sidled into my perceptory as I was weighing up the merits of a caramel flume over a custard log. I tend to attract the attention of chthonic scammers, seeing in me an outstretched leprous hand of need. The man began rambling on the topic of a $100,000 cheque sewn up inside a winged chair in the used furniture shop across the road. He asked me for the £200 needed to acquire the chair, then a percentage of the loot therein. I told him to shove his cheque up his unwiped rectal aperture. All I wanted at that point was a fucking custard log. He then asked if I would help him steal the chair by securing the attention of the serving staff on some contentious issue while he wheeled the chair outside. I told him that a winged chair of that magnitude would need a minimum of two bods, or one large strapping muscle-man, which he was not. I bought the custard log and watched the scammer solicit help from other middle-aged bedragglers as I gnawed into the gooey tendrils of my treat.

As the log was shorn to the last lick, I walked into the furniture shop and purchased the chair, soliciting the help of Tim for pavement transferral, where I tipped it over to plunder the understitching for loot. I penetrated this with a set of car keys, tearing the arse asunder like a psychotic proctologist, as the scammer stared on with hatred. "No cheque!" I shouted. "This man is a fraud!" The scammer coolly reapproached me and said "No, I meant *that* chair," pointing to a chair on the opposite side of the window. Having an ample nest egg of fuck-off funds from the Bergþórusons, I bought the second chair and ransacked the padding for the cheque. The scammer said, "Sorry, I meant that *table*".

I was now in a war of wills with a smart-mouthed asshippo. I bought up furniture, hacked the arses from tables, escritoires, swivel chairs, and sofas. We had attracted a crowd on the pavement as the furniture piled up and Tim ratcheted the prices, knowing his produce's fate. As the last few items were acquired, I made sure to ask the crowd to keep the scammer from scampering. Hacking apart the last table in a mad sweat, having been handed an axe by a local, I shouted, "There! No $100,000 cheque! Liar! This man is a *liar*!" Rather than the rapturous applause I expected from the crowd, the assembled hundreds stared at me with incredulous looks, feasting on that moment of realisation—the moment I twigged that no one had been on my side, rather relishing in my outburst of madness. The scammer stood with a smirk on his face, and I had to be restrained from hacking his hair off.

The police arrived and, there being no crime in smashing up one's furniture on the street, made me hire a lorry to take the ruined produce to the dump. It was hours before I had time for any dinner.

Penmark

"I spit on your pseudo-German Alemannic babble," a spindly man said.

Penmynydd
DREAM [2]: A shedload of manure is unloaded outside the door of my shed. I look towards the large bay window where Helga has her bedroom, and see the shadowy outline of two frames involved in limitless sniggering.

Penpedairheol
Translated, means "someone's sodden walnut".

Penperlleni
I love the pestiferous chic of this village. These morons know their place.

Penpont
Katrin texts: "Hooray! Forty-nine exquisite miles away from your hellacious face."

Penprysg
I am the petticoatted imp of impotence.

Penrhiwceiber
Hill-bound, maroon-skinned and cramponned, I stare at weeds with Katrin. "Isn't life absolutely repulsive?" she says. I sniff assent.

Penrhiwgoch
"Laugh your problems away!" a local twmffat said to me.

"My friend, your simple-minded philosophy is useless in the whomp of cruel reality. This might work in the comatose quietude of the Southern Welsh marshlands, where streaks of human pisswank are no problem, and the rustle of the wind shields you from the devastating sickness of the whole affair. But for me, this rank attitude is nothing if not a self-deluded invitation to further, deeper, soul-sucking misery," I might have responded.

Penrhos

It seems that most people, heaving their burdensome bodies along cold uneventful pavements on septic mornings, wear that impassive face that suggests: "I could evaporate right now and no one would notice."

Penrhos Feilw

Having sunk two vodkas and five scotches, I hopped in the Saab to here. I pissed against someone's railing as an expression of bitter disappointment that I had been outcast in Wales in under twelve minutes. I volleyed the sarcastic wind with a loud burp.

Penrhyn-coch

From *An Alternative History of Wales*:
>   1469 AD: First mandolin invented then burned up for firewood.
>   1657 AD: The night classed as form of weather.
>   1769 AD: Education reforms help educate nine Welsh.

Penrhyndeudraeth

A skulk around the derelict Bron Y Garth Hospital, a former workhouse in the mid-1800s, on the lookout for the famed lesser horseshoe bats. I was startled to see inside an old woman in a chair in the former reception area. "I have a 9.40 appointment. Mrs Armstrong," she said, mistaking me for a nurse. "You might have the wrong building," I said. "I been coming here for over forty-six years," she said. "That doesn't mean you're not a stupid old boot," I said. "What? I been waiting for over an hour now," she said. I stepped for a nonce into the ill-fitting hobnails of power, musing on the implications of tricking this far-gone nonagenarian—whether I should reassure her that the nurse would arrive in a few minutes, leaving her to rot in this airless ruin until she expired, or enter a futile war of words, using the ruinous surroundings as a fulcrum with which to lever my logic into her cooked old conk. I chose to let her expire. She was a symbol of the futility of progress in a world peopled with narrow-minded fussbudgets who like things to stay the same. She was welcome to her ruin.

Penrhys
I eat liver twice a week. A Persian cat meows all the time. The cock crows.

Pensarn
Tanya Donnelly, your attempt at a Belly resurgence with the bloated and unappetising new album *Dove*, was foolish.

Pentlepoir
Overheard:
"I would like to take this moment to mention that Melanie Smithsie is awesome. She wears a onesie, and I cuddle her little shoulders, and I love her quizzical fringe. I am in love with Melanie Smithsie!"

Pentre Gwynfryn
DREAM [22]: The tall man who penetrates Helga has asked me to fluff him before intercourse. I caress the burning helmet with a desire that seems almost criminal.

Pentre Maelor
I observed a po-cheeked youth at a bus stop and attempted a mental sketch. In the evenings he can muster up enough not-so-awful by filling the silence with laughter. When he turned sixteen, he realised that all his years spent watching television and not speaking to people were going to backfire on him so badly he would need a daily course of laughter therapy to get him through this awkward period without the need for suicide or something worse, like talking to his mother. But watching these programmes alone has simply deepened the loneliness that laughter alone provokes—laughing is a communal act sparked by the happiness of others, i.e. if his mythical friends were laughing along with him the laughter would grow from the initial joke into laughing at each other's laughter, until the jokes became irrelevant and his pleasure centred around the act of being together and laughing. So his laughs were never deep belly laughs but a series of amused smiles, from slightly curled lips to big banana grins. Occasion-

ally, when something struck him as particularly hilarious, he would let out a few snorts and involuntary laughs and that would provide the peak of his contentment for the night, with the remaining four hours spent trying to recapture that single belly laugh by watching more and more comedy until nothing seemed particularly amusing anymore. In fact, by watching so much comedy he would learn to turn every aspect of his life into a self-deprecating gag to make it seem less devastating than it was. Rather than confront his appalling loneliness and depression head-on, he'd drown himself in humour, positioning his self-conscious brain voice as an audience responding to his actions who, instead of viewing each blown opportunity and missed moment as an unbelievable failure, would see him as the hero-schmuck of his own sitcom, bumbling through life with his humour and integrity intact. Only there was no audience to empathise with his hilarious suffering except the part of him that took his failure deadly seriously, and that part didn't find the schmuck remotely amusing at all—in fact, the schmuck was laughing at him. So whenever he'd laugh "at himself" to cope with the daily awfulness of things, he'd be mocking the seriousness of his problems so the self-conscious brain voice would give him a minute's respite from feeling like shit enough for him to get through the day and actually do something.

Pentrefoelas

My mother poked her nose into my room as I was reading *On the Road*. She tucked her pencil skirt under as she sat on the bed and said to my fourteen-year-old face: "Son, I have something important to impart. It will be impossible for you meet our expectations. You see, our expectations for your success are already so vast, that unless you somehow manage to perform the work of two or three people in the same space of time as you would the work of one person, you will be unable to meet these expectations. Also, the fact that you know we have these high expectations will put psychological pressure on you, and whether you feel that pressure or not, it will constantly niggle at the back of your mind, and you will attempt to rebel against this parental influence by turning to idle or nihilistic pursuits, or you will have a breakdown and turn to underperforming and prescription medication. Both of these paths will leave us disappointed. You see, there is no solving this problem. You might wonder if me, sitting here now telling you about these expectations is itself the trigger. This is a valid rebuttal. However, I think if you understand now that it will be impossible for you to meet our expectations, our expectations having long ballooned into the realms of the physically impossible, then you should have a reduced neurosis when it comes to meeting them. You will disappoint us, however much you achieve." I nodded. I was for two decades unsure whether this upset me or not.

Then I tried to write a novel and her speech returned to me. Twelve pages in I realised that the novel would never meet my expectations, as my expectations for the novel had already ballooned into the realms of the mythic, and whatever I wrote—whether the novel was of considerable literary potency or not—I would never write the supernovel that existed in my head, and the whole thing would always appear mediocre to me. The legacy of self-sabotage that my mother had left me with those words, in that bedroom, spoken to my fourteen-year-old face, made their full life-crushing impact.

Pentregat

"Bad men need nothing more to compass their ends, than that good men should look on and do nothing," said John Stuart Mill. I say, "What good men?"

Pentwyn

I am the loose-stockinged whore of the night.

Penuwch

Mother: "You are condemned to the life of a twitchy snarling teenager, trapped inside a sagging mass of ageing man, squeezing your boils and smearing your sticky pus upon the sleeves of meekest survival."

Penydarren
A croissant was once eaten here.

Penyrheol
I shot an elbow near an oxbow.

Penysarn
"You have your whole life ahead of you," a man told his son.

"Excuse me," I stepped in. "This is parent-speak for 'To scuttle around in desperation attempting to fill the chasm of a prescripted existence in a corporate dystopia with a futile search for love and meaning and the consumption of alcohol, chocolate, and TV depicting lives far superior and pleasurable than your own.'"

I was punched.

Pisgah
Translated, means "a cloven hoof in the swamp is not there".

Plashett
There is a plaque here on the wall on which Timothy Spall once leaned.

Pontllanfraith
Bergþórusons, one morning the world will awake from its chrysalis of complacence. You will no longer have a place here.

Pontlottyn
I am 10½. I have no cultural awareness whatsoever. I could no more pinpoint a Caravaggio canvas than a Fra Angelico fresco. I am a brainless dunderwhelp. I bike around the icy knolls of my sepia-tinted backwater, swigging tins of Spur Cola, waving at passing cars with a pant-soiling pal named Viktor, and inside the narrow parameters of my cranium, I remain painfully unaware of my class, and my position as an underprivileged oik from a colourless Icelandic podunk. I have no notable acne, and I love East 17, the London four-piece pop combo, whose albums include *Resurrection* and *Dark Light*. When I arrive at their works, it is already kaput for the Walthamstow scamps in commercial terms.

Having arrived five years into their career at the Best Of package, on the backslide from their biggest chart-topper ('Stay Another Day', in which their snowcapped laddish heads forever revolve in my Christmas recall), the record company attempt to sop up the final lucre from their tenure—a prudent slip before the market assault of The Spice Girls and the she-band phenom. As I am hearing songs like 'Steam' and 'House of Love', the band have begun the unstoppable backslouch into their lives as carpenters and plumbers, awaking to the fact their bank accounts are not as plump as aforeassumed.

As I wonder whether coolness and hipness and sexiness will ever be terrains upon which I can pitch a tent and recline (no, as it happened), Brian Harvey, the main singing one, is taking a slow-moving twirl into public madness. He will soon run himself over in a Mercedes having speed-ingested a baked potato, to the merriment of the tabloids, and later, will storm number ten Downing Street, seeking a private audience with David Cameron. Public titters are scarce that time, as the clear undertwinge of undiagnosed mental illness is whiffed on the wind. And Tony Mortimer, bloated and triple-chinned, will turn up to perform intolerable acoustic versions of originals on TV reunion shows, as part of a bleak nostalgia junket. I am 10½. I like their stupid songs 'Hold My Body Tight' and 'Betcha Can't Wait'. I am no more mindful of their impending hells than I am of my own. I am in a blissful state of numbness to naffness, the brutal belching naffness of existence. Is this the closest I ever came to contentment?

Pontnewydd
O, Helga . . . I imagine us in the frenzied slobber of our sexhaving, on the pre-priapic cusp of a mouthful of O, in that sweatdrenchedclench, with pleasure-blank peepers rolling back into our skulls, in that sensational, insufferable O-moment, when the tantalising knowing of tingling bodily pleasures is the only thing worth knowing, when there appears, in our topright eyes, a solo, wobbly tear of love-kissed bliss . . .

Pontrhydyfen

Helga Horsedóttir, for you, I would rustle up a functioning hose from rubber tubing to save a hot kitten in a blaze.

Pontsian

This is what Aaron Swanlopp said to me:

"You might think me a full-on certifiable nutbag for this. But for one annum I chose to become a cupboard squatter. I was someone who squatted in a strangers' cupboards for a whole annum. I entered people's homes through various means: as a dinner guest, a romantic involvement, a gatecrasher, and located the roomiest cupboard I could find. I would then remove from the handbag I had brought a collapsible stool and open up my laptop, where I would spend the evening surfing the internet or running the online website I maintained (about the phenomenon of cupboard squatting). In the daytime, when the owners of the house or flat in which I cupboard-squatted were out, I would have use of their kitchens, bathrooms, and so on, and sometimes in the evenings too, if the owners were at movies or parties. As a consequence, I paid nothing on food or rent. All I had to do was remain discreet and in the evenings, when the owners were asleep, refraining from loud clacks on my laptop, sneezes, coughs, or excessive movements. I became a statue at night and restricted myself to silent clicks and slow typing. To avoid detection when the owners used their cupboards, I chose storage spaces, and tried to hide behind whatever items were available (one time I set up my chair behind a large gazelle statue), but invariably, I was discovered and had to find new cupboards. The owners, upon discovering me, were not too appalled, since thanks to the fast-rising success of cupboardsquatters.net, the practice had become accepted among the public. I simply packed up my suitcase and moved on. I recommend cupboard squatting for at least an annum. It is a relaxing break from life."

Pontyberem

I remember my time in Berlin, lapping at lust like a parched manx, making starved passionless love to a West German prostitute, then seeing my ski-masked reflection in the mirror and nearly fainting with shame.

Pontypool

In Húsavík, men in designer shirts and hand-woven cravats strut along spotless pavements with their pencil-thin brunette wives, their smirking faces and faultless skin on show, a high-spirited sprog humming Dvorak in tow. In Pontypool, men in lager-sodden vests tug their moribund alsatians towards firebombed discount stores to pick up beans and Spam, as their housebound comatose wives slobber indoors before repeats of *Benefit Scum Exposed*. I prefer this hellhole to that one.

Pontypridd

An unexploded bomb pokes from the bingo hall. The falling plaster, and the ever-closer prospect of the bomb either crushing them or blowing them to pieces, is not as important as the splodginess of their markers, which after seven weeks of complaints, have still not been remedied with a softer-tipped alternative.

Porthcawl

One ogreish excess I permit myself is the imparting of brutal truths into the ears of youths. I approached a brown-eyed cherub, having committed his first cliché of pain in losing an ice-cream to the pavement, and said: "This seemingly harmless raspberry ripple sploppage should be viewed, youngster, as broader representation of the devastating losses that you will suffer across your life, and a reminder of how ill-equipped you will be to receive and cope with them." Sometimes I sound like my mother.

Portheiddy

Be afraid, Oman! Icelandic corporate fascism in the warm slippers of liberal democracy is coming!

Porthkerry
I wonder if I will ever leave Wales, and if it matters.

Portskewett
There was a man there, I saw there, running round a field blasting sheep with a fire extinguisher. He might be traumatised.

Presteigne
It is 3.49pm. I am sitting in the Saab with an erection. I have no erotic thoughts on particular local women. Nor even Helga Horsedóttir. I am merely sitting here with an inexplicable erection in a Saab. I am afraid.

Princetown
I met Katrin the seventh time in a Greek restaurant. Over a bowl of tzatziki, she told me that her mother was petulant and unclean.

Prion
Overheard: "Mitchell, I'm afraid I've been lying to you all these years. You aren't my son, you're actually my father."

Puncheston
'One Friend Too Many' from Barrie Bartmel's *Poems of a Poltroon* (p.11):

> Three friends is one friend
> too many
>
> Feeding the diorama
> of their dire dramas
> into the VCR
> of my recall
> is tiresome
>
> Three friends is one friend
> too many
>
> Two friends is one friend
> too many

Becoming the spare wheel
on social occasions
the odd man out in a trio

Two friends is one friend
too many

One friend is one friend
too many

Listening to the same stories
ad nauseam
knowing their quirks to the point
one can predict
their every utterance

One friend is one friend
too many

Pwll

Overheard:
   "I was a miserable sack of maggots and dung for over nine decades. I sleepwalked through existence, feigning pleasure in the things most commonplace, until, one balmy Tuesday, I met Agatha."

Pwllgwaelod

Helga Horsedóttir, for you, I would capture the crazed late-summer wasp, starved and fuming for nourishment, with strategic upturned glass.

Pwllheli

As I ambled towards the butcher to bag a beef olive for dinner, I noticed a youngster vaulting across the road clutching a purloined saveloy in his right hand, narrowly missing a fatal clipping from a Ford Focus in his haste to consume the length of seasoned sausage. The butcher, not accustomed to such wanton pork thievery, and not a man prone to the hot pursuit of meat-starved urchins, followed in bumbling unchase, having to wait for the traffic to subside to resume the pursuit he had barely begun. The thief, meanwhile, mauled the sausage in a frantic attempt to swallow the evidence, eating from fear not appetite, in a backstreet. I followed the fat asthmatic butcher along the pavement to his arrival at the urchin, chewing the last mouthful while innocently texting friends outside a transport caff. From my viewpoint at Boots, I watched the butcher prod the urchin on the back and begin scolding him in a booming brogue. I expected mature threats to call the police or a stern paternal rebuke, and the matter dropped. What I saw was the butcher shove four fingers into the urchin's mouth, prise the lips apart and hold them in a clamp, then insert his considerable schnoz inside, to the point his lips were slobbering across the poor lad's chin. This was done in an attempt to catch the urchin in a lie, to scent the saveloy inside as evidence, however, the petrified lad vomited up the entire sausage across the butcher's face once the nose had been withdrawn. The pork-cheeked meat-peddlar, recoiling from the undigested saveloy like a bullet to the face, exploded, clobbering and kicking the child while howling Welsh swear words that sounded impressive in his mad basso voice. I ran over, along with twelve others, to save the child from a split cranium, and helped haul the butcher against the transport caff wall, as kindly women attended to the crying child.

Before I left town, I learned the local paper had shifted the focus from *thieving urchin* to *insane paedophile butcher assaults seven-year-old in alleyway*, and that criminal prosecutions were underway. As an eyewitness, I could have intervened to help the butcher, but frankly, his meat was substandard, and anyone who inserts their nose into a child's mouth needs several years in a cell to sort themselves out.

Pwllmeyric
You are brimming with rheum, Jim Reid.

Pwllypant
I am the lecherous wasp of the overlands.

Quarter Bach
If this hamlet were a noun pertaining to photography, that noun would be "tripod".

Rachub
Here, a small salmon-shaped man waddles up to one, and whispers, "Pass the hatchet, I think I'm goodkind."

Rassau

> There were three brothers from Vik
> whose business rulings were strict
>   They shared the same head
>   slept in the same bed
> and screwed you with the same prick

Rhigos
In spite of the name, Horsedóttir, "daughter of horse", there is nothing equine in her bearing. She is leonine, magisterial. I wish I had my cock in her hair.

Rhiwlas
Helga, I dreamt that you caught me masturbating over your Facebook photos, and I literally melted in shame.

Rhos-on-Sea
The sun is a big burning liar, offering an illusory, mocking brightness on an insane barren land populated by sunless war-bearing assgibbons.

Rhoscolyn
A cod-liver-scented village riddled with delusional wrinklies hellbent on titivating their snuffage. No matter where one chooses to croak,

whether in a harbour-side villa overlooking placid waters and circling birds, or in a rat-riddled backstreet in a pile of bin bags, that brief unavoidable vista into the void awaits us all. You can convince yourself that croaking in a four-poster king-size mattress surrounded by loving family is somehow a classier, more sophisticated way of entering eternal nothing. But nothing and the moment preceding nothing is egalitarian. You cannot impose your financial or social status, your zeppelin-sized self-worth, or what an overbearing asschaffinch you are on the void. The void eats everyone, equally. I love the egalitarianism of death. It's the kindest thing life has to offer.

Rhoscrowther

I am chewing a pineapple when I recall the opening scene of Joachim Trier's *Oslo, 31. august*, when Anders retrieves a sunken bag from a river, and tries to drown himself while clutching the bag. There is nothing in particular I would like to take with me to the watery abyss.

Rhosesmor

Here, shellshocked families exist inside the remnants of their blasted flats, taking open-air baths at precarious angles, sleeping on burnt mattresses, staring at the fizzling screens of cracked televisions, while their toddlers crawl over bricks and cables, over plaster and mortar, along the emptied bowels of their bombed lives.

Rhosgoch

The Quantum Scale of Facial Catastrophes (in five phases):

Quantum 4—"Rosacea Sunset": You are slammed up in a prison of sebaceous sorrow. A place where inexplicable pustules and pimples, of every size and severity, appear with indiscriminate lewdness on your person—your lower ulna, your middle swathe, your upper clavicle. One morning an explosion of volcanic bumps will appear, an array of popocatépimples, on your forehead or below your hairline, a fencer's paradise that stings to the touch. If you are lucky, you might not suffer from a rampant isthmus of reptilian bacne, nodular acne that renders the backs of chairs no longer relevant to your life, or the pleasure of backside acne, where nodules pepper themselves in awkward phalanxes along your scabby buttocks, and love to hide themselves inside the anal cleft, making sitting down or shitting a thing of the past for you. If you are lucky. And you certainly won't be.

Rhoshirwaun

DREAM [14]: A man with a buzz cut and six-pack approaches Helga's house. Twelve minutes later I have a vague sense that inside the man is behaving with a beastliness that outclasses Guatemala.

Rhosllanerchrugog

Helga, do you remember that night when our eyes briefly aligned? When I arrived, you were waving off you colleagues. I maintained a cool quarter-mile lag while shadowing you along the pavement. I noted how your handbag buffed against your auburn cagoule, suggesting a lightness of contents, and how your stride had a lack of springiness. Perhaps you feared raising your child alone, returning to another evening ministering to the brat's needs, and longed in your heart to hurl her into the waiting waters of the Skjálfandi? Perhaps you wished to snuggle up to a new life, to traduce all memories of your drowned husband, to inhale the aftershave scent of a box-fresh body? (Mine?) Helga, do you remember?

Rhosmeirch

From the parish Twitter: "I urge for the third time that the Big Bish send over the bulldozers. Two wrecking balls from either end should remove this ecclesiastical stain from Wales. This is a prime opportunity for McDonald's to step in."

Rhosson

Helga, here are five things I would do to secure a flecklet of your ardour:
    1. Perform that double bass solo in a swimming pool.
    2. Receive an award for the funkiest tattooed haiku.
    3. Topple a pompous moose.

4. Decide that the link between violence and monkfish is enormous, and write a stern letter to the President of the Sea.
5. Believe in the boring.

Rhostryfan

When pissed, I lose all moral righteousness, and lapse into the role of a humourless burping clown. I tend to crawl along a wall and flick cured meats at passing Skodas.

Rhostyllen

Overheard:

> "I was a bit like no then I was like OK then I was sorta hmm well."

I wish I had that sort of lucid thinking.

Rhosycaerau

'A Soporific Yet Scary Play' from Barrie Bartmel's *Poems of a Poltroon* (p.18):

> Anaes-
> thea-
> terror-
> ised!

Rhydcymerau

From *An Alternative History of Wales*:

999 BC: First settlers unsettled.

753 BC: Battle between the Ordovices and the Geoffs. Victors: the Geoffs.

345 BC: First bowtie made from anthracite. Bowtie exports to the East Midlands make Wales prosperous and hated.

Rhydlewis

This email was sent to me in error:

> You are a repulsive fraudster. I am NOT interested in appearing in your "novel", if you are even writing one.

I clicked on the 'donate' icon in error, having viewed your site with vague interest. After clicking on this icon, I closed the page, having made the mistake of entering my email to "win the chance to appear" in your book. I then received hourly messages, reminding me with increasing aggression that I had not paid the £40 required to "appear" (it was made clear nowhere on your website that this involved a fee). The next morning, I received an email informing me that a "Hellhound Trojan is on your trail", and that the remedy involved paying £40 and completing my "message". Because I am suddenly bombarded with pop-ups linking me to Russian escort sites, and I cannot access a single webpage without being redirected to accident claim scams, I paid the funds in a panic. You then sent me an "antidote package", involving six hours of loading and nine restarts, and I still have some horrible gif on my desktop of a porn actress sucking a large black cock. This is vile, morally dissolute behaviour. I DEMAND that you return the £40, and that you send me another "antidote package", removing that disgusting image. My children use this computer. How am I supposed to explain that vile gif to them? I also FORMALLY REFUSE YOU PERMISSION to use this "message" in your "novel". I am only writing to you in this box since there are no other ways of contacting you. If the above actions are not carried out, I will seek some sort of legal action for the trauma inflicted.

Rhydyclafdy

I met a man who was once a peacock. He occupied a corner of the King's Armpits and was chronically unwilling to talk about his time as a peacock. No one, in over seven years of trying, had successfully prised a sentence from him regarding his time as a peacock, except for the extremely canny reporter from a local paper who first managed to uncover the fact that the man was once a peacock in Watford,

Hertfordshire, and that his name was Franke (sic) Marshm (sic). The actual facts, the concrete, incontestable reasons as to why the man had been a peacock for that period of time in Watford, who he had been cohabiting with (who was his "owner"), and why he stopped peacocking to move to this remote rural Welsh enclave to forge a nondescript and miserable existence in moody pubs, was a question no one had been able to answer with any certainty. Because I showed absolutely no interest in this man once having been a peacock, and spoke to him on a range of non-peacock-related topics, such as the advantages of cooking South Chilean chicken in twelve litres of ghee prior to seasoning, and the failure of the Maastrict Treaty to unite the eurosceptical hard-right with the beleaguered post-communist West Germans, he revealed to me the reasons for his peacock past. Because there was such a curiosity in the village about this, I let the villagers know that he had confided in me the reasons for his being a peacock, and that I would let them know the elaborate and fascinating story in the morning. I sneaked from my hotel around 2.15am, and left the village forever, letting the secret remain, as I will in this report. You will never know why Franke (sic) was a peacock. The one interesting thing about this poor, sad man was that he used to be a peacock, and no one knew why. If the truth ever surfaced, the man would no longer hold interest for anyone. He would crawl into a wretched burrow of mediocrity, and vanish to no acclaim.

Rhydypennau
Translated, means "left to rot on a sinner's hot veranda".

Rhymney
Katrin said: "I encouraged my father's adultery. I told him, 'Your wife's policy of intercourse on birthdays, anniversaries, and special occasions is a form of torture: a sexual Guantanamo. You need to be detained at a pleasure centre, with access to regular anal and oral probings.'"

Rhymney Bridge

"I am Richey Edwards. I parked my Vauxhall at the Severn View service station and walked into Chepstow across the bridge. I was busy appreciating the reinforced titanium bolsters when I heard Chris de Burgh blasting from a Rover S40. I had a moment of 'woah, Elsie!' and hurled the cheese sandwich I was eating into the brine. The tormented polemics of the Manics was not the aural future I craved. I noticed that a de Burgh tribute act was performing in Rhymney Bridge that week and I travelled to see him. Listening to that middle-aged man was like a lightning bolt to the soul. I felt shame at leaving behind the social cred of our rock band. I changed my name to Driscoll Ardent and went shock-blonde. I began working on a new material influenced by Chris. I am content performing these ditties in this bar. It is my destiny. I never particularly cared for the histrionic agit-punk attitude that I helped cultivate, so whatever. I miss Sean, though. That man can drum," Richey Edwards said.

Rockfield

Katrin: "I make a point of purchasing pets that loathe me, like a feral cat rescued from a shitpipe, or a malnourished dog with PTSD, so I am saved from that sham comfort we feel from brainless creatures who would without hesitation snack on our hearts if the meat in pouches were to vanish overnight."

Rogeston

That time I fought two thugs kicking a Somalian immigrant and the Somalian immigrant rose to his feet and punched me in the chest. He had seen me. In the hot sting of his wounded pride, he needed someone weaker to punch to reassert his machismo.

Rogiet

Mother: "You can dress a merchant banker in the rags of a tramp, but in his soul, he remains a merchant banker."

Rosemarket

The people here want nothing. Except that.

Rowen

There is a plaque here outside the church where Boz Scaggs once punched a beadle.

Ruabon

This is what Akiko Grolsch said to me:

"I woke up that morning to a staggering piece of news. Dennis called the house at three o'clock and told us he was a solicitor. We were eating dinner when the message came through and we were too shocked to take another chomp. We had known for a while this might be coming but we had not expected it so soon. Father was the first to speak after a long silence. 'Where do you think he'll go?' My mother shook her head, frowning. 'I guess to a firm of solicitors.' I was too stunned to make eye contact with my parents, so I carefully scrutinised the mash instead. I noticed father had switched to instant mash from his homemade Marigold potatoes. He'd been having a hard time at work lately."

Rudbaxton

I sat on a pineapple for the feels. Subsequent arse-bleed.

Ruthin

O, Helga, I am holding your panoptic forehead as I thrust into you from behind, increasing in speed and randiness and running a finger along the circuit of your sweet lips. I am screwing you over a picnic table as your little girl looks on in pleats sipping a carton of orange squash. Your pale buttocks are vibrating with every twelve-inch cock-thrust I lovingly provide. You clutch the wet wood and capacitate the wet wood I am piling into you harder and faster, murmuring O-O-O in passionate amentia. You turn around, and from the curtain of your flowing black hair, you observe that I am the one screwing you, that a pimple-faced human volcano is inviting his cock into your unblemished and untarnished cunt, and your lust-filled face turns to horror, as you scream the sex away. I run hard-cocked towards the house. Your unfazed little girl sups her squash and says to me: "Hey Quasi, one of your blackheads has burst." She is referring to the small burble of pus at the tip of my cock. You are screaming rape and have covered the entire picnic table in vomit. I awake unsettled.

St. Andrew's Major
I was looking forward to a hot-water bottle, a spin of Nico's *Desertshore* on the ipod, and a thimble of rum in bed, when the B&B owner approached me in the hall with the prospect of a free cider in exchange for enduring his presence for several minutes. I expected the unburdening of some long suppressed crime as the motive, as was usual in these backwaters, when the vacant sump of November compels semi-sane men to spill their pain to foreigners, in the knowledge those foreigners will never visit ever again. I was correct. The owner had learned last month that his current wife, Glenda, was in fact his biological sister, having scratched a long-held genealogical itch to the tune of £800 through *Genes Reunited*. He had passed the point when telling her was appropriate—immediately—making the situation far worse as he continued to not tell her and to have sex with her. The B&B belonged to Glenda, and he had no savings or skills to fall back on. I told him his two options—to either remain with Glenda and learn to live with the biological accident somehow, or contrive an exit strategy, to start looking for alternative employment. Having not told her immediately, and continued to put his penis inside her, she would loathe him however the news was broken. He thanked me for the counsel. Before I left, I handed Glenda a note in an envelope, reading "SORRY, BUT YOUR HUSBAND IS YOUR BROTHER. HE KNOWS AND STILL FUCKS YOU. ALL THE BEST, MAGNUS."

St. Arvans
Overheard:
  "I intend to write about an unnamed man who sets out from his home to purchase a loaf of bread. I am not concerned with artistic

merit in telling this tale—popular aspects in novels such as a striking style, inventive form, or probing character insights. I am concerned with moving the character from point A to point B: from his house to wherever the bread is bought. This novel is an attempt to be ordinary."

St. Brides

Helga Horsedóttir, for you, I would create a kickstarter for a Tuvaluan beat poet seeking to turn his pain into bracing on-stage improv backed with pounding 4/4 riddums.

St. Clears

Bergþórusons, once this is over, I will spend the rest of my days undermining your attempts to heal the world with avocado stone removers, topical-memed onesies, and the novels of Nicole Krauss.

St. Elvis

I urinated on the grave of Dafydd Evans, b.1919, d.1998. Nothing personal.

St. Hilary

Barrie Bartmel was found washed up on a prong two miles west of Rhossili Bay. He was the most misunderstood Welsh poet of his generation.

St. Lythans

I espied the writer Vaughan Grenade hitchhiking on tarmac.

"Get in the Saab," I ordered. He entered.

"So listen. You know I'm working on a new novel?"

"Ah-hah."

"I'm sort of not-working on it now."

"Ah-hah."

"Note the distinction. I'm not *not* working on it. I'm not-working on it, with a hyphen. If I was not working on it, I would be sitting on the sofa staring at three-star Danish noirs on Netflix while shovelling in sweet chilli crisps. But I'm not-working on it, which means although I haven't written a single word for four weeks, I am still writing parts in my head. I'm trying to reanimate a manuscript that has lain lifeless on a mental slab for too long."

"Ah-hah."

"I've reached a crisis point in my non-career as a writer. I've published a couple of books to a thin burble of acclaim, which I accept—I'm a humble-ass brother, as you know, I have never courted notability—however, I feel the perfect form for my words is elusive, that every literary tack I take ends in exasperation and abandonment. Perhaps there is no form for me."

"You've tried linear?"

"I have tried linear. I have written followalongable, readonable, pageturnable, hookandteaseable, and extremely tiresome nuts 'n' bolts prose."

"Hmm."

"I'm looking for a form for my formlessness."

"So what you want is a logical, coherent form for illogical and incoherent content?"

"Yep."

"So the form completely undercuts the content?"

"The form *houses* the content. The form should function like a Victorian asylum. A repository for hopping mad prose, packed inside cosy, padded walls, where visitors can spectate the lunacy in perfect safety."

"Or like the notebooks of some forgotten scribe unearthed from behind the wall cavity of an old bedsit?"

"That's an idea."

"Let me posit this posit. It seems that a fear of being understood is at the heart of this. In seeking a form for formlessness, you wish to present a series of confused, aimless prose yawps as a legitimate form of expression. Rather than working these aimless yawps into coherent cerebral transmissions, i.e. to impart some kind of experience, wisdom, or authenticity, like popular writers do, and make yourself understood as a man in this world, you are purposefully bodyswerving any attempt at participating in the human race. Perhaps you fear that whatever you have to say will somehow appear pathetic, or worse, banal?"

"I praise your posit. I would argue that a refusal to make yourself understood, to position yourself in opposition to the human race, is as valid as writing from experience or wisdom, since I view the concepts of experience and wisdom with deep distrust. A state of permanent alienation and resentment at having to mingle with these flesh-covered buggers known as human beings is as valid a view in prose as overcoming adversity, and learning to love some stuff around you, which is what popular prose essentially tries to teach."

"Hmm."

"The problem with writing in general is realising that whatever brilliant idea you think you have, when scrutinised under a hypercritical microscope, will appear limp and derivative in the harsh unforgiving light. To be a writer, you have to somehow simultaneously engage intensely with your words and ideas, while completely deluding yourself that they are nothing more than rehashed mash in a tramp's bowl."

"To be a writer, you must exist in a constant state of contradiction?"

"Precisely. You convince yourself you write for yourself alone, knowing that you obviously write to be read and published and reviewed and liked and loved or hated and slated. You convince yourself that your book has a right to exist, that your voice and ideas are as valid as anyone else's, knowing that your ideas are probably not as important as the ideas of an oppressed minority, or an actual genius. You convince yourself that you deserve to be read, when you know that most people haven't read a word of Shakespeare since school, if they read any at all, so the likelihood that your words will take priority is pretty low. You convince yourself that if your words can pique a reaction from one single person, then your years of toil will be worth it, when you know that slaving away on a manuscript for that length of time for someone to leave a one-word review ('meh') on Amazon is simply not the respect you deserve for such an investment. You convince yourself that your love of literature over cash is enough for the hours you are spending earning no money, when you know that you could be making cash instead of plonking words on a page like a plonker. You convince yourself that the broader populace is not hostile towards literature that isn't topical, plainly written, accessible, and so on, when you know that the broader populace read nothing and leap on their high horse whenever someone criticises their lack of ambition in making it through one Dean Koontz per annum at the beach."

"I see."

"What's this playing?"

"Teenage Jesus & the Jerks."

"Skronk."

"You know skronk has its origins in Japan?"

"Is that so?"

"Before the 1970s no-wave scene, underground bands in Japan were making trademark skronky sounds, of sheet metal being shorn with buzzsaws, of aluminium in a state of ear-boring shear."

"Robert Christgau coined the term."

"And many Japanese musicians, with the echo of Hiroshima ringing in their ears, came to New York form bands like DNA and Friction."

"So atonal shrieking hellfire is a Japanese musical form?"

"You've heard Yoko Ono, right?"

"Ha."

"Lydia Lunch imposed a kind of traumatic, murderous narrative to skronk with her little orphans running through the bloody snow. I prefer the kind of dark dreaminess that Sonic Youth brought to the skronk realm."

"You're moving away from skronk into post-punk. Skronk is characterised by atonality, by a merciless discordant bludgeoning of guitars to the point your ears ooze a strange orange fluid that is probably part of your neural cortex. If you leave the club without a permanent head trauma, that ain't skronk. Sonic Youth managed to pass skronk into melody, thus killing the essence of skronk."

"Stop saying skronk."

"Sorry."
"In fact, get out of my Saab."
He exited.

St. Woolas

The people here want thinner postmen.

Saltney

Goddamn you, liberal Iceland, you metrolumbersexual manbag-wielding sisterfuckers.

Sandycroft

I have taken to fainting in restaurants. The prospect that food might become so repulsive to me, that each mouthful of spud might taste like the rancid output of faecal beetles, seizes me in a sudden shiver of potential. I am losing weight.

Sarn Meyllteyrn

Overheard:

"The reason we are here, Mr. Portcullis, is not a causal consequence of The Board to ship us into cultural exile. We are victims of our own febrile, unrelenting pursuit of the zeitgeist and the cash ringgit. If The Board had not voted to round us up and ship us to this remote backwater, we would have fizzled out regardless, victims of our own failure to find new forms to express the mores of our age."

Saundersfoot

Be afraid, Niger! Icelandic corporate fascism in the warm slippers of liberal democracy is coming!

Sennybridge

The World Interspecies Kissing Championships took place in Sennybridge. Maniacs from the world over lined up to tongue-wrestle two hundred creatures for six minutes to win various prizes. Victors included a short Belgian man in a stovepipe who approached a chaffinch superglued to a twig for the event, pressing his thick lips against the blue-striped beak while the bird flapped its wings in protest. A striking Romanian supermodel mounted a tame tiger and charmed the beast with her long passionate tongue. A well-built Dutch stevedore placed his lips over the head of a snake and sucked while the cobra's tongue hissed inside his mouth. A retired librarian placed a stepladder before an elephant and, locating the crevasse below its trunk, presented her own thin lips for an awkward pucker. Losers included a Swiss dentist who snogged an orangutang for four minutes before the creature flipped and swung its amusing arms in a hostile "no more" motion towards the man. An accountant with chapped lips was no match for a furious gecko. And a teenage girl underestimated the fighting spirit of a woodpecker, suffering severe top lip damage that required suturing by the on-site doctor. The event was declared by all a success, although protests from PETA have made a repeat event next year unlikely.

Shirenewton
The gentry and not you.

Shotton
DREAM [3]: As I shovel manure away from my shed perimeter, I trouser the thought that the arbitrary cruelty of the human race is either uproariously funny or vaguely arousing.

Sigingstone
'Your Link, Lydia Pink' from Barrie Bartmel's *Poems of a Poltroon* (p.8):

> I clicked on your link
> Lydia Pink
> and I have to think
> Lydia Pink
> that whatever you are paying your shrink
> Lydia Pink
> is not half as much as she spends on drink
> Lydia Pink

Silian
There is a plaque here on the fence where Aung San Suu Kyi once troubled a rabbit.

Six Bells
When we regret, we are saying "I wish I had been another person at that moment, a person who might have yielded a better outcome than the mediocre one I produced". This is moronic. Regrets are little shots of psychic pain at having been born in our own skin. You are better off practicing self-loathing as a vocation like me, you rueful trout.

Skewen
In a Dortmund brothel in 2012, I recall the scene in Andrea Arnold's *Red Road* where a child murderer unknowingly performs cunnilingus on the murdered child's mother. C'est moi. I am the balaclava-clad child murderer of the boudoir.

Snatchwood
Yes, I peered at a traffic cone for one hour. At some point, I slumped.

Soar
Anita Lane is the chronic bankrupt's Marianne Faithfull.

Southerndown
Mother: "Your scowling hurt at the unfairness of things will not serve a warm bowl of justice to the bumfucked hordes."

Spittal
A mother in the throes of a nervous collapse struggles to pull her pram up the kerb, explodes in frustration and for a second strops off towards the pub, leaving her child on the road. She returns following a thorough pat-down of her sweaty brow and hoicks her offspring back into her wobbling universe.

Stepaside
Be afraid, St. Vincent & the Grenadines! Icelandic corporate fascism in the warm slippers of liberal democracy is coming!

Sudbrook Rumney
This is what Terence Opal said to me:

"When I married her I no idea she would abstain from pruning her pubic hair to such an extent a wild, untopiarised bush would erupt down there. One night, filled with spite when she refused to prune to a respectable afro, I splashed a vial of kerosene on her hair and set it alight. The thicket was so dense that when she awoke in the morning the flames had failed to singe a single strand. As the flames crackled in hot ochre undulations, she decided she would keep them. 'Thanks for the kerosene bling, baby,' she sneered at me. Always keen to pioneer off-beat fashion trends, she would 'trailblaze' this one as autumn approached and the reds and yellows fell in season. In my despair, I chose to sleep on the couch in case I was roasted alive at night in my duvet. I reside there to this day."

Sychdyn
Translated, means "caught in the crosshairs of an ailing sniper".

Sydallt
I was handed a wad of toilet paper and told, "Expect weather."

Tafarn Y Gelyn
Translated, means "a pie in the air is no longer edible".

Tal-y-bont
I see: the sun setting on the Húsavík coast as a seal cadaver is pecked clean.

Talerddig
This is what Vaughan Grenade said to me:

"I had toiled in the town for too long on a no-hope novel about no-hope novelists and their no-hope novels. I had occupied a small room overlooking the quivering waves of the Gordon river with the intention of emerging with a career-making masterpiece. As the days past, firing up another microwave meal for one, sinking into the solace of an evening's futon to pour over prose better than the prose I was pounding onto the page, I came to realise that I was writing not a novel against the hopelessness of writing, but against the hopelessness of life itself, and that I had written over four hundred pages mocking the prospect that I, or any other novelist, dared to pretend that they had something to offer of insight about the act of writing."

Talgarth

It was late. I had necked seven scotches and a limeade chaser. In a haze of burp, I recalled in italics the horror of being alive for two hours . . . *the sickening fact that your mother, that monstrous lump who could snap your neck like a twig if she wanted, has chosen to name you Vincent; the pledge you must make to yourself never to show any love or affection towards the sort of odious reptile who, of the millions of potential names available, in all the abecedaries of the world, would think that Vincent was anything other than a violent bludgeoning of your life chances; the homemade blanket with its pattern of bluebells and thrushes, indicating someone in your family possesses a notably poor talent for crocheting; the two hours that have passed without a complimentary Dr. Pepper; ennui as the novelty of the whole "being born" thing has worn off; your annoyance at not being able to form words when in your brain the sentence "I am preposterously perplexed by the nugatory nature of this nascence" is clearly present and longing to leap off your tongue; suddenly falling in love with the locum when you recall the delicacy with which she cupped your head and bum when you wriggled from the womb, and proposing marriage to her with the noise: "aawaawaaawaooahaahaooo"; an upsetting flashback to your previous life as an alcoholic stevedore as you take that first milky suckle of your mother; a moment of nostalgia for your time as a zygote, and the sad acceptance that those days are lost forever; the partial forgiveness of your mother while savouring the seriously sweet taste of her mammilian emissions; the still fairly obvious non-appearance of a male figure known commonly as a father . . .*

Talog

Travel "broadens the mind", the cliché speaketh. Travelling round Wales, it seems, splits the mind into a million frenetic anxieties and manias, some of which lead to cardiac arrests on log flumes.

Talysarn

Yes, I hurled a cat into a shrub.

Tenby

Politically, I am unclubbable. I loathe how the billionaire elites pump their waterbeds with the tears of the poor, and at the same time I hate the ill-read populace, with their willingness to believe foul demagogues, their refusal to break into a sweat learning political concepts, their voting for the loudest arsehole on the platform, their cooing at the "honest" candidate who says "I will fuck you all" to their faces. I hate the chattering classes, with their sham concern for the lower orders, when their situations never budge an inch with new leaders or policies. I cannot choose between hating the cunning of the amoral ruling classes, the pig-ignorance of the thick-headed, or the twittering of the bourgeois at their wine-tastings and vegan brunches. There are no parties for the sane-minded misanthrope like me.

Thomas Chapel

'A Dentists' Xmas Party' from Barrie Bartmel's *Poems of a Poltroon* (p.20):

> Dance
> the
> bossa-
> novo-
> caine!

Tir-Phil

From the parish Twitter: "I urge that Bishop Wilson consider the closure of this parish. No one attends masses here. It is a waste of funds keeping this place open. I suggest a larger parish is opened in a more central location like a town. Thanks."

Tir-y-berth

It occurs to me, as I sip eggnog through a straw, that Helga has a minute, perceivable pimple on her neck. If I returned to her a preened, pimpleless man, might that one blemish stoke a loathing in me? Or, if she were dermatologically inferior, might she develop a complex, and yearn perversely for the repugnant old me? In other words, could even the memory of my condition ruin my chances with Helga forever?

Treffgarne

Be afraid, Tajikistan! Icelandic corporate fascism in the warm slippers of liberal democracy is coming!

Trelawnyd

I was almost punched when I said the last Catatonia album is a wambling snotball of an LP.

Ton Pentre

Trust nothing in these "reports".

Tondu

Ironworks and suspicious deaths.

Tonyrefail

This is what Norman (???) said to me:

"My name is Norman and I am a skier. You don't believe me, eh? No, there are no skiers called Norman. I know, I know. This is a fiction. Do you see how simple it is for fictions to collapse? The simple suggestion there might be a skier called Norman is too large a suspension of disbelief for the listener. Plus it is a lazy notion: setting up a name and an occupation to suggest the real. Far better to commence in the act of something trivial or unique. For instance, my name is Norman and I am taking a shower. I have dropped the soap on my right foot and am awaiting the sudden spasm of pain to throb in my tootsies. There it is. I hop up and down and then slip on the soapy water, banging my head against the towel rail. I am dead. See, that's a step too far. You can't begin a story if your narrator dies within the first few sentences. These are mistakes practitioners of fiction do not make. Take note, Ben."

Trawsgoed

'That Song' from Barrie Bartmel's *Poems of a Poltroon* (p.4):

> I played that song
> that sent me spinning
> into a montage of my
> unspectacular and pedestrian
> past
>
> where for 3:26 I am transported
> to a rose-tinted paradise
> with my fictional self
> skipping across elysian streets
> of fictional history
>
> and afterwards I wrinkle my nose,
> put on Rammstein,
> and order is restored

Trearddur Bay

It is strange arriving in a new land. The overwhelming need to commit some repulsive act to shame and blacken Iceland makes me incapable of civil discourse. To bitch-slap a benevolent uncle stricken with curvature of the spine. To rut with a plump librarian on a knoll in the pissing rain. To circulate a handstitched periodical espousing fascist Macedonian invective. To torch a campervan with two basset hounds still inside. To compliment a mother on her newborn, then let rip a fart on his face. To purchase a rare edition in a book shop, then rip the book to pieces before the weeping seller. To blast Electrelane from a bluetooth speaker as a procession honours the Welsh war dead. To wipe one's arse with the bride's wedding dress. To gargle cullen skink in a restaurant until the police are called. To wolf-whistle the hotties in a cancer ward. To whisper an incorrect statistic into the ear of a fact-starved child. To turn up dressed as Sarah Palin at a wake. To moonwalk in a museum. To list a toaster as 'new' on ebay when the stack is all crumbed to hell. To secrete a small microphone under one's tongue, take a seat at the movie screening, open up the first bag of poppadums, and began chomping. To criticise the petunia's rhizome in full hearing of her cousin. To harrumph when the mood has changed from rumbustious dissent to patient acceptance. To spoil the view from a lakeside cottage by erecting a large billboard showing the advantages of CSS Grids over Flexbox. To create a hostile atmosphere in a B&B over lunch by walking up to everyone's table and warning them not to order whatever food is on their plates. To slap a Boer. I considered these things. Time was ample.

Trecwn
Overheard:
    "Hello again! We met at the benefit to raise money for osteoporosis. I quaffed too much of the complimentary Pernod and unleashed a little vomit over Zadie Smith's shoes! I spoke to you about my novel, *Summer's Witness*, and we discussed the possibility of you "putting in a word" (I hate that phrase—whereabouts does one insert this word?!) for me at the Franklin & Merchant agency. I have the manuscript ready to send (after a last-minute retyping emergency—an incident with cat litter and Ararat!), only I need your email address so you can forward it on to them. I hope you don't mind me contacting you directly. Is £40 the fee? I wish you well and apologise for boring you that night!!!"

Tredegar
If this town were a liquid, it would be mango-flavoured still water from Oldham.

Tredomen
The people here want a one-disc edit of *Sandinista!*

Treffynnon
I have this imagined conversation where I say, "Father, you are a boring Icelandic cipher," and he says nothing, because I am correct.

Trefnant

Overheard: "Mitchell, before the last rites are read, I should tell you, you're actually not you . . . you're me. Sorry about that."

Trefor

"Life is fun!" a man told his son.

"Excuse me," I stepped in. "If your idea of fun is perpetual war, famine, corruption, injustice, unfairness, cruelty and irrational hatred on a second by second basis, then you might have a point, you grinning prune."

I was not punched.

Tregagle

A car, hazards ablaze, in a sump off the B4293. No one around.

Treharris

My leaving the parental home at seventeen—the acme of acne—was the right time. I could sense that these people, having had the tethers of their love snapped with the first purulent zit eruption over supper, needed space to focus on Kerri's prettiness and potential and zitlessness. I recall the lies in their eyes when I picked up my suitcase, and the taxi arrived. "You can stay," my mother said. I paused for five seconds. Her face in that five-second pause was enough. I moved into a bedsit and started snorting meth.

Treherbert

Helga, here are five things I would do to secure a flecklet of your ardour:
1. Seek employment in the seediest nooks of the Seattle underworld.
2. Claim renewal when no renewal has taken place.
3. Wrap a rap CD while rapping about wrapping a rap CD.
4. Become Swiss in seven steps.
5. Dropkick an otter.

Trelech

Mother: "You might have noticed, Magnus, that I never cuddled you throughout your childhood. I also instructed your father to avoid affection or reinforcements of love and warmth. There was a reason for this. You see, studies have shown that sons who receive a surfeit of maternal cuddles end up viewing women as vapid snugglebags who exist as emotional cushions for bruised male egos. Similarly, sons who receive a surfeit of paternal pride end up as a strong patriarchal she-slappers, viewing women as interchangeable walking vaginas. It is better, if we are to fight this scourge, that men are shown no bias from either parent and are encouraged to punch themselves free from the paperbag of patriarchy."

Treoes

The music of Margo Guryan keeps me sane. The paintings of Roland Penrose keep me sane. The writings of Hubert Selby keep me sane. There is only insanity, without art.

Tresaith

Elegance and decadence. Tresaith endless.

Trethomas

There is a plaque here outside the laundrette where Zoe Wannamaker once washed a muddied cagoule.

Trevethin

Crag-bound, shoe-footed and rain-pocked, I stare at a cluster of people fussing over a fallen elder. "Isn't life a sack of sad smothered aardvarks?" Katrin asks. I cough assent.

Trimsaran

Translated, means "a pub caulked with bigots".

Troed-y-rhiw

I am weeping in a field. I have a lemon in my mouth.

Twyn-y-Sheriff

I wonder if I could write a novel that sounds like a thousand men screaming.

T Croes

The Quantum Scale of Facial Catastrophes (in five phases):

Quantum 5—"The Merrick": You are The Elephant Man. You are barred from a circus sideshow for scaring the freaks. You are a walking tumour, a reminder of the staggering imperfection of our damaged species. You will never experience love or compassion. You will forever be viewed with extreme revulsion and horror. You will spend most of your time in isolation, whether self-imposed or at the behest of the authorities. You will have to come to terms with life as a total outcast, as an inhuman thing that people wished would vanish from the Earth forever. You will probably commit suicide at some point, which without seeming unkind, is probably the best way to spare you a lifetime of pain.

Undy

Helga Horsedóttir, for you, I would cross the road to prevent a brutal man from clobbering an owl.

Upper Boat

I bumped into the Scottish man who loathed the crime writer Ian Rankin.

"Last time, I was explaining how—"

"Yes, I remember. Proceed."

"Rankin-Rebus's Edinburgh is an imagined place, one where the middle-class Morningside-dweller can imagine a sordid and sexy underworld inside in their squirearchical, punchably pretty city, and romanticise about the pea-souper mystique of R.L. Stevenson, the blueprint for this (and most other) fictitious versions of the capital. The raggedy outskirts aside, pitching a dark detective series in Edinburgh is akin to situating a hotbed of sleazy criminality on the streets of Kensington or Chelsea. The real sordid underworld of criminal ooze exists in the podunk towns and villages, in the un-picture-postcard perfect places. Rankin's twinning of scenic Edinburgh with stabbed dudes and evil shenanigans allows the reader a snug backdrop from which to indulge in their violent rubbernecking while the real crimes take place in unpleasant, socially bereft backwaters that readers would rather not visit textually, or actually, among desperate and impoverished people. The brooding darkness that Rankin strains to cultivate in books with fistable titles like *The Naming of the Dead* or *The Impossible Dead* or *Dead Souls* (pinching from Gogol is a hangable offence, with apologies to Ian Curtis) is in fact couched in a romantic fantasy of Victorian Scotland (a fantasy the Scottish literary world has been milking for touristic not artistic purposes for a long time). Rankin's novels have become an unwitting wing of the Auld Reekie tourist industry, and in his undeniable role as a corporate, establishment, cash-hoovering man, Rankin has long lost the kind of outsider rock-and-roll cred that he desperately strives to maintain, playing in third-rate dad-rock bands with broadsheet journalists to prove to his audience he is still that plucky young punk from Cardenden underneath. The Rebus novels are nothing more than fat tourist pamphlets, crammed into bookshops and libraries, and no matter how many Rolling Stones album titles he pinches, no matter how much indie cred he tries to claw back, the fact remains that tours around Rebus's Edinburgh can be purchased, proving the man is in shameless cahoots with The Man. Rankin is the establishment figure young Scottish writers should be kicking against with violent, knifey jackboots."

"Yeeees. I suppose we must plunge into the old discussion about populist art propping up outsider art. No Rankin, no unknown innovative new novelists. Bestsellers enabling poor-selling yet interesting new fiction."

"We could. Except there is no innovative new work. There's Rankin. There's Rebus after Rebus after Fox after Fox. There's DI Tinwhistle, DI Pocklochie, DI Carsehole, DI McStabber, DI Switchblood, DI Hamfisted, DI Buggeringshitweasel. There's crime publishers and crime publishers and crime publishers. There's Hackface

Books. Strangle the Kitten Publishing. Babydrowner Inc. Bang Bang Stab Stab Press. There are no other publishers. There's one insane, unstoppable exploitation of a population's seething bloodlust, a nation lusting for war and conflict who flock to libraries to read about the immoralities they are desperate to commit themselves. There is a population barely holding the veneer of their lives together, as they sit and stream cop show after cop show after cop show after cop show, then stuff their brains with cop novel after cop novel, in the hope that some of that sexy evil makes their monotonous peacetime lives passable, until the time comes they can pick up a bayonet and ram it into someone else's guts, like their whole being is screaming out to do. Yes, crime writers, you think you are exploring the frightening labyrinths of human psychology, you think you are plumbing the *la bête humaine*, when you are really showing your own murderous cravings, and stirring up a nation's lust to maim and stab. You are architects of evil and your souls wallow in an amoral sewer (except on Twitter, where you speak out against moral injustice, in order not to alienate your audience)."

"I'm not touching that."

"Allan Massie's assertion in a fawning *Telegraph* article in 2015 that 'crime fiction is real literature' seems like the sort of thing someone who writes crime fiction would write if that person considered themselves above crime fiction and was irked when reviewers failed to praise their crime fiction written for cash in the same manner as their literary novels. (Or a better version of that sentence). Rankin was created in collaboration with Aberdonian novelist and critic Massie in the late 1980s, when the latter said to the former: 'Do you think John Buchan ever worried about whether he was writing literature or not?', and has remained one of Rankin's most prominent cheerleaders. In his article slapping down genre-baiters, Massie dismisses the inferiority of crime as 'palpable nonsense', then cites Walter Scott, Dickens, Dostoevsky, and Gide as examples of crime-as-literature (though these are writers of *literature-with-crime*, not the current churners of product, and in what respects the mediocre 18th Rebus novel *Stand-*

ing in Another Man's Grave compares with *Crime & Punishment* in the literature stakes is a question too perplexing for this feeble snobbish brain to compute). You can't merely mention authors who wrote about crimes in their works and then place Ian Rankin and other crime writers in their ranks because they write about crimes too . . . this is madness, this is a criminal rationale, this is to conveniently bypass every brilliant sentence written by Dostoevsky *et al* in contrast with the hacky third-rate ones written by Rankin *et al*. Madness!"

"Hmm."

"Massie then states that crime fiction has the edge over literary stuff, because 'he [sic] can range over [sic] all levels of society, for crime breaches the barriers of class'. Massie's summation is that modern literary novels 'tend to deal with one layer of society', 'with people all leading the same sort of life'. This assertion pleads ignorance of the rich seam of literature featuring characters from all sorts of backgrounds, some from varying layers of society in the same novel, i.e. it seems to ignore literature. The article then makes the usual 'duality of the city' reference (RL Stevenson) switches into a promo for the Rebus novels, throws in a Latin phrase (translated, of course, since the writer is not a snob, although it is snobbish to assume that we wouldn't understand the Latin phrase ourselves and need the trans). Essentially, the case for Rankin as literary literature is not made, because there isn't one. The case that crime fiction is literature is an open one. However, crime writers have to start writing it. Rankin has to start writing crime fiction as literature. You can't write sentences like 'She seemed to have given up the steak and was dabbing her mouth with her napkin' and expect to be bumping uglies with A.S. Byatt and Henry Miller. If these writers stopped worrying about readers, audiences, publishers, demographics, formulas, balance sheets, critics, then their heads would be clear to write literature."

"Enough! Put the hatchet away! You and I both know this all stems from lust."

"I admit it. As I stare at the Google images of Rankin, usually peering at the lens with a mischievous smile before sweeping Edinburgh backdrops, his boyishly unkempt scissor-fringe piercing the tufty black brows, I realise I am looking at a man half of whom I will never be, I will never be that humble colossus, posing in Edinburgh pubs with Sandi Toksvig or Alan Yentob, that I will never have more than three results on the "images" page, that I will never pose with random readers in adoring selfies, that I exist in an interzone between interesting and uncommercial, and extremely bizarre and uncommercial. I am a nervy hypochondriac with no flair for living. Mr. Rankin has succeeded at life."

"Finally, an honest statement!"

"To end. Crime fiction is our means of imposing a kind of existential order to our lives. Crime fiction is a kind of moral elixir. The crime is, usually always, solved. To refuse the reader a resolution is to infuriate the reader. The crime writer, then, is in the business of reassuring people that the villainies perpetrated on the planet are always rectified. That the moral scales are always equilibrized. The crime writers themselves would be the first people to admit this is cobblers, and that evil prevails more than niceness. In that sense, these crime novels undercut their explorations of evil by offering the reader the resolution they crave, these writers are spoonfeeding the people false optimism. And there is nothing worse, carping reader, than having to open one's maw and swallow a spoonful of hope."

"I applaud your bleak candour."

"Thank you, chum."

"I hope I never bump into you ever again."

"Diddums."

Upper Cwmbran

If this suburb were a self-help book, it would be *The Weight Loss Cure "They" Don't Want You to Know About* by Kevin Trudeau.

Upper Redbrook

The lower part is in Gloucestershire.

Uwchmynydd

"We know that most people are eugenicists in their hearts. We know that most people value the athletic over the autistic. We know that most people would eat the cripple first when the plane went down. We know this. We introduce equal rights programmes and positive discrimination to suffocate the guilt. Regardless, we know that in our hearts we believe that the quadriplegic would be better off dead, that those with severe special needs are half-people. I am hated because I speak this aloud," Katrin said.

Valley

I suppose you Bergþórusons had something more like a travelogue in mind. A droll encapsulation of the locale from the smarm-tongued lips of an ethnographically naive foreigner, buttoned up tight in a cloak of knowingness, like the works of Paul Theroux or Bill Bryson. Not short paragraphs of me pissing on Cambrian railings, accounts of post-lunch masturbation in a Saab, or erotic reveries involving a divorcee who is probably an insipid bourgeois mongoose. I suspect you Bergþórusons will not read this. So I will continue to chronicle these relaxing pisses on private land, in the interest of truth.

Vaynor

I suppose I should provide some ethnographic information for my paymasters. This village has approximately 3,500 people to patronise and infect with the contagion of Icelandic culture. You might have a hard time shafting Dylan Thomas from the canon and replacing him with Halldór fucking Laxness.

Walton East

I am caressing Helga's milk-white bum and stroking her wet clitoris when the moment arrives to penetrate her. I open the lovemaking with a series of slow, scrumptious swivel-thrusts, enacting a circular motion with my penis as I luxuriate further inside her marvellous vagina. I tongue her spine, caress her ink-black hair, and vanish into interstellar bliss with closed eyes. When I open them to admire her bum some more, at the bedroom window stand my colleagues from the Húsavík Research Institute, wincing and laughing and pointing as I pleasure a purring Helga. I meet their scorn with a series of more intense and passionate thrusts, until Helga turns around to reveal her head transformed into a three-headed replica of the Bergþórusons, who fix me with a stare that means "get out of our cunt". I am unable to withdraw. My cock is irretrievable as the brothers begin to smirk and smirk and smirk, and my colleagues increase their wincing and laughing and pointing. I wake up perturbed.

Waterston

'Redbird' from Barrie Bartmel's *Poems of a Poltroon* (p.21-22):

> I am the contest winner.
>
> Every day, I walk the sands to find fragments—a barnacled conch, a crunch of razor clams, a wash of shells—for pieces of the puzzle. How, in this misted world, is it my fate that I, of all mortals, won the writing contest?
>
> On the horizon, I observe Crispin walking towards me with his slanted brows, his tussled blonde crown. Crispin calls me redbird. He says there is always a fire in my head. He says that short paragraphs with untaxing fauxpoetic language always heat up the panel. He calls me the wounded sparrow too.
>
> I listen to the sound of the waves. Nature, red in tooth and claw, also plays well, Crispin says. And well-known literary references. Crispin is wise. He often sits upon the rocks and brays at the sun. It is something in his past. We smoke in silence.
>
> It occurs to me that short ambiguous sentences with a mysterious air also yield a certain magic. The inelastic moon hangs low, solace leaden in its dark heart. An allusion to unspeakable emotion caused by past trauma also

works. Inside those waters, a hint of old fear, a sparkle of past pain. My heart afloat upon a wave, rocking the curve of her name. No one among us could feed such starved beauty.

Crispin says the past will bury us, unless we fight. I look to Crispin and withhold tears. I take the £500 prize money, and sketch another scene. A clifftop, at night. A figure with porcelain eyes stands, arms outstretched, reaching for that First Novel Award. The wind in our ears is only the beginning of tomorrow.

Watford
Sheds aflame!

Wattsville
I tend to nap around 2.30. I wake up sweat-creased and sick-tongued.

Wern y Wylan
I see: a yawning East German prostitute with two nicotine patches per arm.

Wernddu
I am the stuffed apologies of discourse.

Wernyrheolydd
I said a thing in a place that no one understood.

Whelston
I have this imagined conversation where I say, "Bergþórusons, you are a triumvirate of talentless middle-managers with blimp-sized egos and your cocksure conceptual mouthswill is poisoning the universe", and one of them says, "You need to unshake the fever dream", and I say, "That means nothing. You are three men in suits making up faux-poetic utterances to impress the imaginationless masses and bleed corporate grants from the fundaments in charge," and one of them

says, "Enplug thou withering seeds," and I release an infinite stream of sick from my throat inside which they perish.

Whitebrook
I started loathing my father in my late teens. I could sense that his paternal love had long passed into paternal stoicism in the face of my face, that his evenings were spent masking shame and contempt. He had always told me the truth. His creeping coldness towards me was the ultimate betrayal.

Whitewell
My mother was a militant feminist who encouraged women to spurn the beauty routine. She herself had never worn makeup. When I turned sixteen, and the pimples of the underworld erupted, she began turning her back when I entered rooms, speed-eating her meals at the dinner table, and pretending to read books whenever it suited.

Wilcrick
Eating a cress sandwich atop the Iron Age hillfort, I mused on whether Liz Phair's unexpected volte-face from cult adult indie into commercial teen-pop was in fact a feminist statement more powerful than the slacker-snark iambs of *Exile in Guyville*. As the rain came on, I concluded probably not.

Windmill Hill
Before these reports progress, I should clear something up: the narrator of these reports is not based on me.

Wiston
Be afraid, Papua New Guinea! Icelandic corporate fascism in the warm slippers of liberal democracy is coming!

Wyllie
Katrin said: "I encouraged my father's adultery. I told him, 'There is nothing much to life except periodic humping. The periodic hump is the reason most people refrain from hurling themselves from

skyscrapers or on to train tracks, and if you are being deprived, then *ce n'est pas juste!*' "

Y Rhiw
It is said that CeCe Peniston once visited here. The occasion has long passed into legend.

Ynysawdre
Bergþórusons, one morning the middle classes will spread their diarrhoea over the walls of your overpriced apartments, set fire to your mid-range twin-powered hatchbacks, piss into your skinny espressos and milky lattes, and leave the city to wallow naked in a bog with ecstatic smiles on their faces.

Ynysybwl
'Your Failed Redraft' from Barrie Bartmel's *Poems of a Poltroon* (p.12):

>A rewrite
>A self-flagellation
>A reduction
>An improvement(?)
>An exhumation
>A forced futile stab at finality
>A war on the past
>A public humiliation
>A self-help seminar
>A self-hate seminar
>A précis
>An indulgence
>An indulgence
>An indulgence
>An indulgence
>An indulgence

Ystalyfera

The people here want a proper socialist government who prioritise the poorest members of society, tax the richest, and work to achieve universal concord and order. (Kidding! The people here want to lock up smackheads).

Ystrad Meurig

From *An Alternative History of Wales*:
>   1982 AD: Aluminium made illegal in parks.
>   2009 AD: Flesh hammocks for ravenous lethargic dogs invented.
>   2042 AD: Bacteria from Neptune found in Offa's Dyke.

Ystradfellte

I was having a nice time potholing until I remembered Idi Amin.

Ystradgynlais

I am spooning up couscous when I recall that moment in Thomas Vinterberg's *The Celebration* when Christian mentions his father's sexual abuse in a casual aside at a lavish familial reception. I hope one day, I will have the courage to address my family and let them know they are repugnant, spineless asscockerels.

Helga Horsedòttir

I was sitting in a Skoda with Katrin. I was heading to the hospital in Reykjavik, where my mother was lying in a bed attached to drips.

"What are your thoughts on her impending death?" she asked.

"I'm torn between wanting to feel compassion like a proper human son should and looking forward to not having to listen to her patronising remarks ever again. I'm torn between the loathing I feel at having no real feelings of compassion towards her, or feeling a single thing when I picture her suffering through chemotherapy, and the fact that she intentionally raised me to feel these things for her book's sake, and married a man with a wonky genetic line who I hold responsible for me turning into an unlovable creep. As usual, the burden of balance and thought is utterly clouding my right to make binary judgements."

"Your mum's a legend. She simply laid the groundwork for a future where men are subservient. She's trying to create form of emasculated non-man free from the murderous stabbing time and cockramming of most male men."

"Without my permission. For an entire childhood."

"Do you seek a guinea pig's permission before you blast him with chemicals for the sake of progress?"

"We're here. Exit the Skoda."

I strode into the hospital and rubbed the thought "phew, at least this isn't another intolerable room populated with snarling curs" for a mo. The proximity to dermatology wards, the nearness to dying people, created a lovely levelling between freedom from facial tyranny and the fear of premature death at my own hand following years of ceaseless facial tyranny. I lingered in the corridors, eyeballing the terminal, extremely happy it wasn't my turn to lie on a trolley with tubes up my nostrils, then went to find my mother. Fresh from a blast of chemotherapy, she had withered seriously since the last I saw her, her head like a dried apricot, her body an aspirated sack of organs and bones. She was sat upright holding one of her books.

"What are you reading?" I asked.

"*The Putsch of Ssshh*. It's being reissued by the University of Delaware," she said. Her voice had lost none of that self-assured utterness of its self. "It's my study of women who use silence to rebel against their dominant husbands. How they can turn the power dynamic to their favour by creating a hostile, tense environment in the house. Hello, Katrin."

"Hello, Mrs. Mínervudóttir."

A silence followed that was not a pleasing reflective silence that families who feel—for whatever inexplicable reason—comfortable in each other's presences have at such significant moments. This was a silence that spoke of two people who had wandered straight back into the chasm between them in under two minutes, a silence made worse with the pressing need for a sort of summing-up of the mother-son union to be made.

"I'll be dead in a few weeks," she said. If I loved one thing about her, and I didn't, it was her knack for boring straight to the fucking point.

"I know. Is there anything you want me to do?"

"No, I have everything taken care of."

"All right." And another silence opened up where I was supposed to express a sense of sorrow at her imminent passing, where I was meant to find soothing words, where I should speak something to minimise future therapist bills, but I could see she feared the exact same threat of enforced tenderness I feared at having to enforce, so I looked to Katrin for help.

"I read your novel, *Like a Burning Swan*," she said.

"Thank you, Katrin. It was sorely underappreciated by the press at the time. Unfortunately, Icelandic literature has never migrated far from the self-mythologising pastoral mode."

"I need water," I said, and let the moment die, to everyone's relief.

❈

The prognosis of several weeks presented a problem. Since I lived five hours away from the hospital, the trip was inconvenient within a certain time frame—perhaps one or two weeks would be considered excessive for a mother who was not beloved—however, if she hung on for three or four weeks, there was no reason not to make another trip to visit, beloved or not, where the last words would have to be uttered. I toyed with an unburdening of my peeve at her parenting style, perhaps in the form of a polite critique as per feedback on a peer-reviewed paper, but all my feelings had already been articulated when the book was released and panned in almost every journal, in far more precise emotional and psychological terms that I could have managed. It would be simpler to present her with a serious of cuttings, place the plastic wallet on her lap, and say, "There. Góða ferð!"

As I keyed in the code for a chocolate nub, a tall lubber with a suitcase came shagging along the corridor sporting a coppice of chin tuft. He stared at me as we passed, then kept staring at me as I passed even more, then stared longer when I continued passing and he stopped.

"Hello! Excuse me?"

"Yes?"

"I couldn't help noticing your ailment," he said. It was impossible to see his lips through the oral shrub. "My name Borvil Girasson. I won't take up much of your time. I have been speaking to doctors about my company's insurrectionary new cream. Can I expand?"

"Expand."

"Thank you. Our cream is called Spotless. It is a brand new miracle cure used to treat nodular acne, like yours. We have tested our cream on over thirty sufferers, and all of them have experienced results in the first five days. Would you be interested in trying our new cream?"

"I so fucking would."

"Marvellous! Please, feel free to pocket a complimentary tub. You are to massage the affected areas twice a day. The lotion contains ichotar, poxterine, and monkicide, and might cause stress or hallucinations. You are not to take this cream if you are allergic to potassium."

I took the tub and smeared an immediate streak across Mark Gardener. Having tried several hundred other miracle creams, I had no problem larding unusual chemicals into my skin without googling their side-effects. I had tried creams made from frog spawn, the sweat of calamari, re-augmented hops, starched flannel sop, petrolatumult, reversed Swiss bog water, coal tarpaulin, armadillo piss, the products of canaries, and swerved rusting.

"That's right. Rub deep, my friend. OK. I have an appointment in Gardabaer. Take my card," he handed me and shagged off along the corridor. It was time to return to the dying mother.

※

Katrin said "I hate-tweeted Michelle Obama" and my mother said "I raised Magnus to feel knock-kneed at the labialicious splendour of the cunt" and I said "Icelandic socialism is a front for old-world colonisation" and Katrin said "I sometimes fuck strangers in vans" and my mother said "I regret every single time I let myself be penetrated" and I said "Our ruling elites are using liberal lies to forge a new slave trade" and Katrin said "I spend a lot of time masturbating to beefcakes stroking their balls on webcams" and my mother said "The female orgasm should be performed in private like a sacred ritual" and I thought "I really, really wish I had my cock in Helga's hair" and somehow we all survived the hour without crying.

"You realise she'll be dead in a week?" Katrin asked after.

"She said a few."

"She extended the deadline so you wouldn't have to fumble an affectionate farewell."

"Oh."

"You could call that an act of love."

"Hmm."

※

The following week, I schlepped around the Research Hive muttering "hell pockets and snapped biscuits". I scowled at women. I lusted after Helga's saucy shanks. I scowled at men. I exchanged barbarities with Katrin following passionless, passive sex. I waited for my mother to die. I scowled at swans. I taunted Lionel Shriver. I reheated old hatreds in a sizzling mental wok. I ate spaghetti and chitlins.

Then, at the end of the week, squinting into the mirror for the usual pustule status report, I noticed Kevin Shields had entirely receded. I poked with tweezers at the spotless, smooth skin-surface, pressing hard to check he wasn't lurking in a knoll of cheek-fat or awaiting peekaboo beneath an earlobe. I went to sleep worried. I had nightmares that Kevin Shields would return to engulf my head. In the morning, someone had burgled my face. All the spots—all of them— that was Miki Bereyni, Bilinda Butcher, Rachael Goswell, Liz Fraser, Adam Franklin, Yuki Chikudate, Andrew Sheriff, and the rest of the purulent crew, had vanished. I stood staring at the mirror for an hour. I couldn't choose between laughing or screaming or weeping, so I opted for a weird mixture, the sort of noise a clown might make if he was being simultaneously amused, dumped, and stabbed. I touched the bumpless plane of my pale face. I rubbed and rubbed and pulled my hands away for fear the spots might pop back, then rubbed again. I shaved my beard. I spent three hours staring at my spotless, blemishless face, too astonished to have a single thought that wasn't "Uunnuuu".

Then I cried like a fucking child.

※

In a spontaneous, butterleggèd attempt to behave in a manner befitting the new me, I put on the herringbone three-piece I had worn to my father's funeral, hit the pavement with a contrived swagger, and leapt into a cocktail bar. "Bring me a fucking expensive mojito," I said to the waiter, looking him in the eye, looking him in the chin, looking him in the torso, looking him in the crotch, looking him in the knees, looking him in the toes, looking an ant in the antennae. I fumbled around the silk-lined pockets for my mobile, made an Instagram rictus, and took twelve selfies. A man with a zit on his chin walked past and a wave of unbridled self-contempt surged up inside me, a feeling of room-swirling panic and fear that forced me to make a lunge under the table. I was trembling. I was spitting nouns like "ostrich" and "filigree" into the heated imperial marble floor. The waiter from whom I had ordered the fucking expensive cocktail called "sir?" and "sir?" and "sir?" as I kicked against the spewing and fainting impulse. In a sweat I came up, asked for a bucket of water. The waiter brought a pint and I swallowed the pint and ran back home and I ran a bath and I sat in the bath for two hours and I cried some more and I ate cinnamon. Later, in a Radiohead tee and unwashed denims I shuddered along the frost-faced streets of Húsavík like a man accused of a crime involving children's pants and hoarding krona in Swiss vaults. I swore at a nimbus. I ascended a hill at a dangerous speed and descended panting. I had another shower. I bumped into Katrin coming home from wherever she had been. "What the facial fuck?" she said. I said nothing. "New cream," I then said. She ran inside and up to the bathroom where she found the tub and slathered the miracle cream across her pocked features with the zeal of a starving urchin shovelling free fennel into his maw after a week of want. I prepared for life as a normal man through a process of walking and staring at people. I met the eye of a man in a smart shirt and caught myself unthinkingly lowering my head. I told myself, "You are no longer ashamed. Your face is a placid desert of bumpless beauty." I walked on. I met the eye of a man in a pair of beige breeches and felt my head pulling. I told myself, "Your face is a hotel bed with satin sheets liberally dusted with cocaine." I met the eye of a beautiful woman with flowing black hair. I leapt across the road and hid behind a pedal bin. This would need some work. I composed myself and continued the walk. To the chortling male in Welsh khakis, I said "I am physiognomically equivalent to you, sir." To the walking male in mauve loafers, I said, "My smooth phiz marks me as a total equal." I repeated this process until my assurance levels hit medium.

✺

I returned home to Katrin. Her pimples had not cleared. A notable redness had appeared on her worst ones, especially Mobutu Sese Seko and Joseph Kony (she named hers after African warmongers). "How long until I see results?" she asked. "Several days," I said. I flexed a muscle.

"I am feeling obscenely confident. It's like someone has mainlined vitality into my pores. I feel like my turds should be put on show in an art gallery. I could kick a tramp in the street and people would applaud. My rendition of 'Range Life' would shoot up the charts and remain for nine weeks."

"How wonderful for you," Katrin said. "When are you leaving?"

"Soon. Remember we made a pledge that if either of us lost our spots we were entitled to drop the other like an infected egg."

"I feel nothing except irritation and expectation that this cream will too render my turds Turner Prize-worthy."

"Good."

"Bear this in mind," she warned, "now that you're sitting on a plateau of countenancial normalcy, you will probably experience a ballooning of misanthropy, a burning resentment at the world for liking you now that your spots have cleared. The sheer, stinging shallowness at people you have experienced for so long, and their pathetic weaselly backtrack into an appreciation of your phiz *now* that it is visually acceptable, is something that will nag at you into the wee hours, however much you are revelling in your new life. You will struggle to hold conversations with people without a mouthful of expletives. Whenever you are eating squid parfait with rich folks, or ploughing some hot bitch, you will feel a surge of implacable hatred in your heart, and that hatred will never, ever, ever, ever, leave you."

"Yeah maybe," I said, admiring my face in the TV.

✺

All that remained was to approach to Helga Horsedòttir and ask her to kiss my sexy, loveable skin. To show her my face, to show her my pretty, unblemished face, and await the outpouring of love she would have for me instantly. I approached her house in my immaculate herringbone and Gucci loafers. I noted the ambulance. I noted her crying child in the arms of a paramedic. I noted her lifeless corpse on a stretcher. I noted the neighbours whispering "suicide". As I walked away, I felt precisely nothing. I felt zero emotions. Whether the emotion was sorrow, elation, or mild nark was irrelevant. I felt none of them. I caught the eye of a girl looking on across the road with pretty red hair, pretty freckles, and pretty dimples. She was prettier than Helga. I sauntered over to her, smiling my beautiful smile, and said, "Sad, isn't it? . . . What's your name?"

M.J. Nicholls is the author of *Trimming England, Scotland Before the Bomb, The 1002nd Book to Read Before You Die, The House of Writers, The Quiddity of Delusion*, and *A Postmodern Belch*. He lives in Glasgow.

BLANK PAGE BOOKS

are dedicated to the memory of Royce M. Becker,
who designed Sagging Meniscus books from 2015–2020.

They are:

IVÁN ARGÜELLES
THE BLANK PAGE

JESI BENDER
KINDERKRANKENHAUS

MARVIN COHEN
BOOBOO ROI
THE HARD LIFE OF A STONE, AND OTHER THOUGHTS

GRAHAM GUEST
HENRY'S CHAPEL

JOSHUA KORNREICH
CAVANAUGH
SHAKES BEAR IN THE DARK

STEPHEN MOLES
YOUR DARK MEANING, MOUSE

M.J. NICHOLLS
CONDEMNED TO CYMRU

PAOLO PERGOLA
RESET

BARDSLEY ROSENBRIDGE
SORRY, I BROKE YOUR PROMISE

CHRISTOPHER CARTER SANDERSON
THE SUPPORT VERSES

CPSIA information can be obtained
at www.ICGtesting.com
Printed in the USA
LVHW020528160622
721378LV00004B/423